THE VALKYRIE'S VIKING

BOOK 1: THE VALKYRIE OF BIRCA SERIES

TANYA NELLESTEIN

wine&words

First Edition March 2021

Cover art by Jacqueline Hayley
www.jacquelinehayley.com

Editing by Kelly Rigby
www.writewithkelly.com

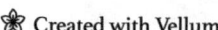 Created with Vellum

For Aiki Flinthart
May we meet again in Valhalla.

PROLOGUE

*T*he silence of the forest had a sound of its own, dense with unspoken secrets. The sudden flight of a bird echoed as if dragons hid in the trees. It's birdsong, a faint, ethereal melody. Creatures, both mystical and real, peered from their hiding places at the golden-haired girl who could already wield a sword better than most men.

Brenna exhaled loudly, refusing to let her imagination overwhelm her. Vali was the one who saw enemies hidden behind fallen trees and in trickling creek beds. By joining in his imaginary quests, Brenna was simply keeping him out from under the feet of the huscarl as they trained. Getting onto almost twelve summers in age, she assured herself she had outgrown these childish games and only continued out of loyalty to her best friend.

Vali had taken off at speed when he spied the illusive enemy hiding in the pine trees, leaving Brenna to guard the pile of smooth rocks they'd declared to be silver. She'd not argued at the allocation of her task. Even though pretend, she had no appetite for attacking without cause.

The canopy of trees kept the forest cool as the sun

blazed beyond their make-believe kingdom. Distant bird-song kept her company. Sitting on a fallen log, she practised balancing the hilt of her sword on the palm of her hand. The breeze came out of nowhere, surrounding her, whipping her hair across her face. Whispers bounced off the trees.

The sword clambered in the dirt as she jumped to her feet. Twisting each way, she looked for the source and found naught. The birdsong seemed to have been swallowed by the forest; only cloying silence greeted her.

"Vali?" Her question was strangled by the unease winding its way around her spine.

An echo of words she could not discern whispered past her again. It seemed even the trees leaned in closer and tighter, trying to catch the words before they trailed off in the wind.

She stumbled against the log behind her. Her heart galloped in her chest as though a thousand tiny horses were trying to escape an unseen terror. She sent a silent plea to Heimdall to spare a moment from his task of guarding Asgard to come and keep her safe, as she crouched to collect her sword.

"You need not fear me, Brenna Ragnarsdotter."

Brenna turned all around, searching for the unfamiliar voice. The empty space mocked her. Turning back to where she started, a vice-like fear gripped her heart, pulling the strength from her bones. Standing just beyond the reach of her sword, stood a figure shrouded from head to toe in black, only his dark and decaying mouth visible beneath the cloth.

The Seer.

"What are you doing here?" She forced bravado into her speech, determined not to show fear.

The ancient oracle lived in the caves above Birca and she'd heard no talk of him travelling to Fornsigtuna.

"I go where the gods direct me."

Her eyes darted around the dense foliage, as if evidence of the gods would appear.

"They are here; the gods are everywhere, child."

His voice was low and echoed off the deep, green leaves and dark tree trunks, crowding in on her. A shiver ran up her spine.

"They see you, child. The gods are watching you."

She cursed the fear that stole her voice; a glare settling on her face to compensate.

"The gods have a message for you."

Somehow, the Seer now stood much closer to her. She held her breath, gripping the hilt of her sword tighter.

"You, Brenna Ragnarsdotter, will fulfil the destiny of your ancestors. You will heal the scars that run deep in their veins."

The invisible vice reached inside her chest once more, squeezing so tight she could not speak, could barely breathe.

"You will rule in the place of your ancestors. The gods have fated it so."

The vice around her heart and lungs let go and she fell to her hands and knees, gasping in the sudden abundance of oxygen.

When she raised her head, the Seer was gone, leaving only his words engraved on her heart.

1

BIRCA - AD 820

*B*renna released the breath she'd been holding. Her husband had lived twenty-four summers more than she and smelled of decay, as though the blood of those he'd slain had taken hold deep within his pores. He continued to paw at her breasts while grinding against her. All to no avail. His cock remained disinterested, as always. Despite the stories he told of his many conquests, he'd never been able to satisfy her as a wife should be satisfied. Or how she'd grown accustomed to with Vali.

Tarben rolled off her, reaching for his trousers and yanking them up. Her husband of only six full moons stalked across the bedchamber; his battle-hardened body bathed in firelight. Brenna sat up, pulling the furs over her body.

Tarben poured himself a horn of beer and continued his tirade.

"You should be with child by now." He tipped the horn back, beer dribbling down his grey and copper-streaked beard. "Instead, my cock withers at your touch. Be you witch, or the concubine of Loki?"

Brenna hoped her shudder of disgust wouldn't fuel his rage any further.

"Husband, I am neither witch nor concubine." She moved off the bed and reached for her shift, pulling it over her head and down her shapely body. "Mayhap it is you who has displeased the gods-"

"Nei." Spittle flew from his lips and fury flashed across his eyes. "I'll see you dragged to Hel by the goddess herself before I let you finish that thought. Valhalla awaits my arrival."

"Not if you die of old age in your bed," she muttered, knowing the jibe was childish and unjust. She sat heavily at her dressing table and began braiding her flaxen locks. This exchange played out night after night, and Brenna grew weary of the blame he placed on her for his failings in the bedchamber.

Tarben's horn missed her head by a hair's breadth and broke upon an oak beam. Brenna stifled a yawn, and continued to braid her hair. He may be old, but he was still a fearsome warrior. If Tarben had meant to hit her, he would have.

"I'll find another, more accommodating bed to rest my head," he huffed, wrapping himself in his fur before stomping from their bedchamber and through the great hall.

The stillness that his departure created left a void Brenna found hard to fathom. Though relieved she did not have to endure his attempts at lovemaking, she respected him as a warrior and his position as Jarl - and she was no happier about the state of their marriage than he was. She had hoped to have earned his confidence as a wife by now. To have him seek her counsel on matters pertinent to his rule. However, his inability to bed her created problems beyond their bed chamber; it relegated her presence as barely tolerable.

Needing to clean the smell of her husband from her skin, Brenna went in search of her maid. Pulling her fur around her shoulders, she made her way to the kitchen, hoping to find Gita, her maid, still at her work. Although she was the Fru and mistress of Tarben's home within the great hall, she rarely set foot inside the kitchen. Standing at the doorway, she was reminded why. Gunhilde and two slaves were tidying the last remnants of the evening meal away.

"Fru, what is it you want?" Gunhilde all but spat at her. The older woman had worked for Tarben since he became Jarl of Birca some ten summers ago. Her dislike of his choice of bride was evident in every interaction Brenna had with her.

Brenna swallowed, refusing to be intimidated by the servant. "I was looking for Gita."

"She's to her bed already."

"Oh..." She did not want to wake the girl. Although a slave, she was the closest to company Brenna had in Birca, and her slumber was well-deserved.

"Can it wait 'til morning, or shall I send a boy to fetch her?" Gunhilde's tone did not bother to hide her disdain for her mistress.

Brenna set her shoulders and her mind. The older woman *would* do her bidding.

"Nei, Gunhilde, do not wake her. I require a bath. Have it brought to my bedchamber and fill it with hot water."

She turned on her heel before Gunhilde could recover and refuse the direction. Not even the old woman's indignant scoffing eased her mood. She was tired of being nothing, a mere trophy to the Jarl and of no consequence to his people.

Within moments, the slaves had delivered the bath and began the task of filling it with water heated over the fire in the kitchen. Gunhilde did not appear, yet Brenna knew she would be filling and carrying buckets with water to the fire; that knowledge giving her a small sense of satisfaction.

"Tell Gunhilde to bring me fresh linens," she ordered the slaves.

"Ja, Fru," came the response without eye contact.

When the bath was finally filled, Brenna lowered herself into the delicious heat and allowed her thoughts to roam freely.

Her sigh echoed around the bedchamber. This marriage had been made at the request of King Aric, and her parents had been in agreement. Having been raised to be fierce and follow her head above her heart, Brenna always thought she'd have some say in her future. At the time she'd thought her father indifferent to her wishes. Her mother had been the one to make her see the sense in the match that was arranged without her prior consultation.

"Brenna," her mother's gentle voice had interrupted her tirade. "Of course, the King and your father would choose your husband. Your father is the King's closest friend and his chief huscarl. The match he has chosen for you is an honour, as much as it is an advantage for you."

"An honour?" she'd argued. "How is marrying a man more than twice my age an honour? What advantage does this bring me?"

"Birca is the gateway to the Eastern trading routes." Her mother had placed her hands on her shoulders, the touch grounding her. "This is an opportunity to rule with your husband; to turn Birca into the most important trading centre in King Aric's land."

"To live the life that was stolen from your family," whispered Brenna, seeing the connection between her past and the Seer's prophecy from all those moons ago.

Her mother's smile had been sad. "My life is as it should be."

"But you are the rightful heir and Queen of Gyldarhagi!"

"Hardly the heir. I was cousin to Princess Ingrid. Nevertheless, my claim died with my family. You and your father are all I need." Hertha regarded her daughter thoughtfully. "But what of your dreams, Brenna? You fight as well as any warrior, yet you have no heart for raiding."

"I will always defend my King and my people."

"Ja, no one would argue against that," agreed her mother. "But we both know you would not be content as a wife unless there was purpose to the match."

"Surely I should judge the value of the match?"

"And who would you choose?" Hertha forced her to meet her eyes. "Vali? What would your life be with him? He will not give up the sea. And what of you? You either join him on his raids, or wait for him while you tend his animals and keep his house."

Her mother had spoken the truth. Vali may have her heart but his dream was not the life she wanted. So, Brenna had agreed with her King and parents, and taken solace in the hope that this marriage would give her the chance to rule alongside her husband, and love would eventually grow between them. That the gods had fated this for her - the Seer had told her.

The water was warm and comforting, although she wished she'd remembered to ask Gunhilde to bring some of the rose oil to perfume her skin. She reached for the soap and lathered it over her body, trying to wash away her memories, both recent and from long ago. She'd believed the gods would have smiled on her for embracing the path laid out before her. Now it seemed, she'd been mistaken.

Brenna shook the melancholy from her shoulders as she rose from the water. Wallowing would not change her situation. Tomorrow she would finally visit the Seer in the caves above Birca and ask him if the gods had changed their mind about her fate.

2

---

*T*he gentle lapping of the water against the longboat coaxed the tension from Vali Hrolfs-son's body, although sleep continued to elude him. The stars lit the ink-black sky, assuring him peaceful passage through the night. They were two days sail from Fornsigtuna and the crew were eager to return home and see their women and families after six full moons away. Their boats were laden with gold and treasure and Vali knew their homecoming would be celebrated; the wealth able to purchase new furs, tools and food for the coming winter.

"You sleep less the closer we sail to home."

Vali turned his head towards the soft-spoken voice of Frode, his long-time friend and brother-in-arms.

"Sleep is a luxury reserved for the old and the dead."

Frode snorted. "All hail Vali, the wise man of the sea."

"I know what keeps you from sleep; visions of Nissa waiting for you in your bedchamber," Vali chuckled, refer-ring to Frode's flame-haired lover.

"You stay away from my visions."

Vali pushed himself up and they sat in companionable

silence, listening to the ocean whisper it's night song. Around them, men slept under oiled skins to protect them from the chill that had crept into the air some weeks back.

"You would be an uncle by now?" asked Frode.

"Ja, if all went to plan, Siri would have a babe in her arms."

"And another in her belly if Hagen had his way, I'm sure."

Vali shook his head. "I cannot believe my sister married a farmer."

"And not a man of the sea? I can believe it." Frode pulled his fur over his shoulders. "Your father died on a raid, leaving naught but you to provide for the family. And you were at sea as soon as you could wield an axe."

"What of it?" Tension knotted his spine. He'd always stood by his choices, ignoring the fears of others so that he could follow his dreams and provide for his family.

Frode shifted in his seat, while his eyes stayed locked on the sea. "I cannot blame Siri for wanting her husband in her bed every night rather than praying to the gods for his safe return month after month."

Acid churned in Vali's gut. He did not blame Siri for wanting her husband by her side either. His hackles rose because of who *wasn't* waiting at home for him.

Brenna.

His constant companion since childhood; his lover and the woman he'd expected to spend this life and the next in Valhalla with. The wife of the Jarl of Birca.

The familiar taste of betrayal and anger rose. He had never expected her to spend her life praying to the gods for his safe return. Nor was that what he'd offered. She was every bit as strong a warrior as he. Together they would have ruled the seas, raiding foreign lands for their treasure.

Discovering more of what lay to the west. Exploring the exotic worlds that lay to the east. With Brenna by his side, nothing could stand in their way.

Vali thought she'd wanted more. And Brenna had. Just not the life he saw for them. She wanted to rule the land, protect the people. He shook his head, still disbelieving her reasons. After what had happened to her mother and the royal family of Gyldarhagi, Vali thought Brenna would be the last person to bind herself to one land and one title that could so easily be taken from her. She'd chosen a lifetime of waiting to defend something, rather than go with him and take the riches that would provide for her people. It was the dream of a fool.

A less than subtle shoulder barge from Frode interrupted his rising frustration.

"Don't waste your time thinking of what cannot be."

Vali shrugged in agreement. "She made her choice."

"Well now, I wouldn't go so far," began Frode. "I believe King Aric made the choice."

"Brenna didn't fight it." Frustration underscored his words.

"To what end? The King made the match and her parents agreed. Who is Brenna to fight that?" Frode shook his head. "Were you expecting her to defy her King and run away with you?"

Vali didn't reply. That is exactly what he wanted Brenna to do. He'd always believed they were fated, that the gods meant them to be together. But she had turned her back on him without a fight. She hadn't even told him to his face that she was leaving.

"Your anger may have served you well in battle these past months, but there is no place for it back home," said Frode.

Vali sighed. His friend was right, his mother and sisters deserved more than his misplaced temper. It was time to put Brenna from his mind, once and for all. Memories of her might still linger in Fornsigtuna, but he would be saved from having to see her, knowing she would never be his.

He clapped Frode on the back. "And I thought I was the wise man of the sea?"

"On most matters, you are," he chuckled. "We should sleep."

Frode rose and made his way soundlessly back to the space he'd made for the evening's rest.

Vali settled back onto his fur, pulling the oilskin up to his chin. The snorts and snores of his crew harmonised with the night sea, eventually lulling him into a dreamless sleep.

3

The distant call of the battle horn invaded her dreams. For a moment, she thought she was home at Fornsigtuna and fighting beside her father and Vali once more, rising to defend her homeland from invasion.

"Fru Brenna, wake up."

She gulped in a lungful of air, dragging her from her dreams and up from her bed. The servant girl stepped back, eyes wide with fear.

"What is it, Gita?" She instinctively reached for trousers and tunic rather than an overdress.

"We are under attack. Warriors in drakkars flying the flag of Sigurd the Black."

Brenna's pulse quickened. She'd faced this bloodthirsty army on more than one occasion in defence of Fornsigtuna. "Sigurd failed in his attack on King Aric and now he comes here. Does he think we are an easier prey?"

Having never raised a sword alongside the people of Birca, she prayed they were not the weaker side. Pulling her boots on, she reached for her leather chest armour. "Help me with this."

She raised her arms for Gita to tighten the straps. "How many boats?"

"Not sure, mayhap two?" The girl grunted in effort as she pulled the straps tight.

Sliding her dagger into its sheath, Brenna took the shield Gita held out for her, then snatched her sword from its resting place. Two longboats could hold over one hundred warriors each. She prayed the people of Birca were ready for such a large attack.

"Take cover, Gita. If Sigurd's men make it to the great hall you must run. Hide in the mountains until it is safe to return."

The girl nodded, eyes shining with fear. "I'll pray to the Allfather."

Brenna turned from the girl and her fear, stretching her neck to either side, thumping her sword against her shield. She left the bedchamber and made her way through the great hall. A nervous energy coursed through her body, which she caught and channeled into the battle-hardened shieldmaiden she was.

I am ready, Odin.

"Fru! Where are you going?"

Brenna started at the booming question. One of Tarben's warriors, dressed for battle with axe drawn, blocked her exit from the hall.

"It is customary for those that cannot fight to take shelter in the mountains when under attack."

Anger ignited. "I am the daughter of the King's chief huscarl. Of course, I can fight!"

The Viking looked her up and down. Brenna rose to her full height, daring him to say more. He shrugged before continuing on his way.

"Dunga," she cursed at him under her breath.

She ran through the predawn toward the bone-shuddering metal of clashing sword and axe. Sigurd's men were already ashore! Battle cries roared in bitter harmony with death screams. Brenna leapt up onto a large rock on the other side of the marketplace and surveyed the scene before her.

Two longboats were anchored at the mouth of the fjord. The tide was low enough that the invaders had been able to wade into shore undetected, catching Birca asleep and unprepared. Warriors fell into formation but the farmers and merchants stumbled about without any direction as to how to defend themselves or the town.

The last of Sigurd's men came out of the water to join the battle at the edge of the village. The blood-thirsty attackers were always easy to spot with their black shields sporting an eagle in full flight, painted in yellow. Sigurd and his most trusted warriors were even easier to find; their eagles were painted in gold. Not that she could see any of the golden eagles reflecting in the dark.

The voice of her husband rose above the fight, barking commands at his men. To the left of the village, where there were fewer longhouses housing traders and vendors, the warriors of Birca had formed a shield wall that was preventing the enemy from pushing in any closer.

A blood curdling scream pulled her attention to the right. A mother knelt in the mud, the body of a lifeless child cradled in her arms.

The screams of women and children, higher in pitch and jagged with fear, rose above the battle cries. A second shield wall protecting the longhouses of the townspeople had collapsed, leaving the families who had not escaped to the mountains in the path of Sigurd's army. A warrior raised his axe and swung it into the back of the mother as she held her child.

Nei!

Her screaming stopped and Brenna felt the woman's silence echo across the battlefield. What kind of monster kills so indiscriminately? Neither the woman nor her child were a threat. Her fury unleashed itself from deep within, carried into being by the guttural scream that sprayed from her mouth.

She ran at the soldier standing over the murdered mother and her child. She swung the sword above her head and brought its full momentum down on the arm that carried his axe. Blood sprayed around her and she hacked at the arm again. As he swayed towards the ground, Brenna kicked him in the chest, forcing him back. Dropping her sword, she put all of her weight onto her shield as she drove it into his face, feeling vengeance surge through her body.

A small dagger lay near the outstretched arm of the slain child. Mayhap the girl thought herself a shieldmaiden. Brenna placed the blade in the child's hand, laying it across her chest in readiness for Valhalla. She rested her own hand on the mother's shoulder, whispering a prayer to Freya for her safekeeping in the next life.

The smell of smoke drew her attention. Pulling her shield free, she reached for her sword. Fire had been set to a longhouse. The enemy was giving chase to the women and children trying to flee.

"*Rassragr*," she hissed.

4

*S*he had to do something.

"You!" she reached for a warrior stumbling back from the melee. "Get a message to the archers to fire on the enemy pushing into the village on the right."

He stared at her blankly. Brenna may not be the Jarl but someone had to protect the people. She must stop the slaughter. She yelled into his face, shaking the young Viking's shoulders until understanding registered in his eyes.

"They are burning the longhouses and killing the women and children."

"Ja, I'll go." The warrior, hardly more than a boy, ran towards the archers.

Sheathing her sword, Brenna retrieved her dagger, running towards the closest of Sigurd's men. She plunged it into the neck of one, pulling it free and dispatching another man before either realised she was there. With barely time to draw breath, she caught sight of an invading warrior running at her. She ducked and stabbed him between the ties of his chest armour. Still, he did not fall. Desperate to win this fight, and her life, she returned her dagger to her belt and drew her sword. Brenna hacked at the Viking until he dropped. Relief flooded in with the oxygen she dragged into her body.

The metallic tang of blood permeated the smoke, suffocating the sea air. Two more warriors headed her way and she added her own war cry to the terrifying roar.

She raised her shield to block the first blow, hacking her weapon forward. The intuitive rhythm of battle replaced conscious thought. Blood spatter painted her face as she worked her way closer to the longhouses.

Bodies fell on both sides in a rolling carpet of death. The enemy was relentless, but so was she.

As the sun crept over the horizon, she finally saw Birca's archers taking their place on higher ground.

"Take cover," she screamed. "Shield wall!"

Her cry was echoed amongst the warriors and in seconds their shields covered them from the incoming arrows. The thuds of men falling to the ground as metal rained on timber shields signalled the sudden attack from the air had hit their mark.

"Attack!" Brenna bellowed.

The roar of bloodlust grew louder as those who fought on found new determination to secure victory. Brenna heard her own guttural howls. She swung her sword, finishing a man with her shield against his skull once he'd fallen to the earth. Villagers worked to douse the flames and save the longhouses, while children scrambled to safety in the mountains.

"Retreat! Retreat!" came the call from Sigurd's army.

She hacked her sword across the face of a young fighter. With victory in sight, she was determined that as few warriors as possible lived to attack them again. Another came from the left, moving too fast to swing his axe with any chance of purchase. She pulled her dagger free and plunged it into his neck. Her shield met his face with a satisfying crack. Retrieving her sword from the ground, she hacked her way closer to the men heading towards the waiting drakkar boats. Arrows flew through the air, piercing the backs of the retreating army.

The cry of victory erupted from the banks of the fjord, rising into the wind that caught in the sails of their enemy and carried them away. The adrenalin of the fight reignited in elation and Brenna stood on the edge of the marketplace and raised her sword, blood dripping from its blade, to the sky. The gods had smiled on them this day.

THE REJOICING of the people faded as Brenna took stock of the human carnage. Her smile began to falter. She let her sword and shield fall to her feet. Fingers flexing to relieve the cramp; her arms throbbing with the aftermath of her efforts. Wisps of trepidation ran up her spine.

The thrall of triumph was barely an echo now as the rising sun exposed the toll of the battle. Beside warriors, women and children, farmers and traders - all unaccustomed to battle - lay maimed and mutilated. None had hesitated when called to arms, still her heart ached for the brutality they'd faced.

As she scanned the village, a new fear wound itself around her core. Walking towards the other end of the marketplace, she searched the faces of the living.

"Where is Jarl Beinersson?" She walked in a slow circle, straining for sight or sound of her husband.

"Fru?" The voice was low, reaching across the field of dead and dying. "He is here."

The Viking's eyes were solemn, holding Brenna's gaze until his true meaning became clear. Her heartbeat thundered as though Thor himself was hurling his wrath across the sky. She fought for air as her chest constricted beneath her blood-stained corset. Dread sat like a rock in her belly, turning her legs to water.

Behind the warrior, the Seer appeared. He surveyed the scene; villagers and warriors waiting.

You must come to your husband.

The Seer's voice sounded in her head, jolting her forward. Sending a silent prayer to Thor for his bravery to guide her, she squared her shoulders. Head held high, she moved toward the Seer. The eyes of the people weighed heavily upon her. As the wife of the Jarl, the Fru of Birca, she must behave accordingly. She paused in front of the ancient one draped in a black cloak, only the bottom half of his face visible beneath the hood. He looked no different to the last time she'd seen him, almost ten summers ago.

"You wanted to ask the gods to reveal your fate," said Einar, the Seer. The air rushing from her lungs as her innermost thoughts were laid bare. "As you can see, you are wife no longer."

She followed his gaze to the body of her fallen husband.

"Lo, there do I see my Father," the Seer began reciting. "Lo, there do I see my Mother and my Brothers and my Sisters."

She fell to her knees in the blood-soaked mud beside the man she'd married. Tarben's lifeless eyes stared past her.

"Lo, there do I see the line of my people back to the beginning."

Her fingers trembled as she reached for him.

"Lo, they do call to me," Einar's voice rose higher. "They

bid me take my place among them in the halls of Valhalla where thine enemies have been vanquished."

She closed his sightless eyes, a single tear sliding down her cheek for the Jarl she had not loved, but respected.

"Where the brave shall live forever."

Her hand dropped to Tarben's chest.

"Nor shall we mourn but rejoice for those that have died the glorious death."

Leaning closer, she whispered, "You were right, Husband. Your place in Valhalla was always assured. Tonight, you will feast with the gods."

*T*he bath was warm, soothing her aching body and heavy heart. With the blood washed from her hands and face, Gita poured water over her head, rinsing the stains from her hair. Brenna sat, lost in her thoughts. The battle playing over in her head; the clashing of steel and breaking bones. Flesh ripped open and eruptions of blood tainting the air and earth. Her husband; dead.

She did not think Sigurd knew of Tarben's death, for he had laid no claim to the jarldom. Brenna had dispatched a rider to King Aric that morning; hoping he would return before the sun rose on the day after tomorrow with word of what was to be done to protect Birca against further attack.

The villagers had worked through the day, building the funeral pyres for the dead and cleansing the town of the stench of battle. The pyres held the bodies of the victorious dead. Each warrior laid out with sword in hand, in preparation to become the Einherjar, Odin's first-rank warriors in the great battle to come: Ragnarok.

Brenna had stood alongside the other noblemen and women, bearing witness to their journey to Valhalla.

Earlier, Sigurd's men had been taken away. Slaves labouring to dig a burial plot large enough for the dead invaders outside of the village. Only rocks would mark their grave.

Now only the body of Tarben remained, waiting for the King to lead the funeral to send the fallen Jarl after his men to the Golden Hall of the Allfather.

"What will you do now?" Gita's voice dragged her back to the present. She was alone with the servant girl, as was her habit. She'd made no friends in which she could confide, and none had seen her as a useful ally in dealing with Jarl Beinersson.

Brenna didn't answer, floating her fingers through the water. What could she do? Her fate was not hers to determine.

"They wait for you, Fru, in the great hall," said Gita.

A chill washed over her, despite the warmth of the water. Her purpose in her marriage to the jarl was to provide him with heirs. With Tarben dead and no heir in her belly, she had no purpose here.

"Do they wish to see me gone from their town so soon?"

Gita's hands stilled from their work. "Fru?"

Brenna twisted to face the girl. She'd allowed herself to be numb, knowing she had no kin nor supporters to call upon in Birca. Still, she had hoped they would not dismiss her so readily.

"I think this town does not wish to claim me now my husband is dead."

Gita shook her head, kneeling closer to the bath. "Nei, everyone saw how hard you fought today. It was you who saved many of our women and children from the axe of Sigurd's men."

Her brow furrowed at this new perspective.

"They are saying you are the reason our enemy is gone and our lands are still our own." Gita grasped Brenna's hands between her own. "You appeared like a Valkyrie sent from Odin to protect us; none who crossed your path survived."

"I did my duty," she began.

Gita nodded. "Ja, you were duty-bound. A duty bestowed on you by the Allfather himself."

Brenna sat back against the bath. Was it possible the people of Birca would not be so quick to return her to her father? When she'd called for the archers, she was acting on instinct alone; she didn't realise anyone knew she had given the command. The only thing she knew for sure was that sitting in the bath would not bring her the answers she sought. She gestured for Gita to finish rinsing her hair.

She dried and dressed, selecting the turquoise overdress that matched her eyes. Gita braided her hair back from her face, pinning it in place with the jewelled comb Tarben had presented to her on their wedding night. Her marriage may not have been a happy one, but the comb reminded her she had entered it in good faith. Regret that she had not tried harder to be a more pleasing wife tugged at her heart.

Finally, she draped her fur across her shoulders.

"It is true," whispered Gita. "You are Valkyrie."

Brenna considered her servant; her awe was evident. Still, one slave's admiration was not necessarily the measure of Birca's warriors and traders. It was time to face her husband's people and discover what the gods had in store for her now.

She entered the great hall alone.

The room was filled with warriors, women and children, farmers and traders. Many more were gathered outside. At the front of the hall, near where she stood, were representatives of Birca's council. Brenna knew they held the balance of power until the King arrived to determine the future of his trading centre.

Feet shuffled on the timber floor as the people rose to greet her.

She lifted her chin in acknowledgment and forced her breathing to steady. Whatever these people thought of her, she would show no weakness. If asked to leave, she would insist it be the decision of the King. She stilled the tremor in her hands by joining them in front of her.

"We won a great victory today." Thankfully, her voice did not betray her, ringing strong and even.

"Thanks to you," said Ubbe, an accomplished warrior, as well as nephew to Jarl Beinersson.

She bowed her head, acknowledging his regard as one of the members of the Jarl's council.

"But it did not come without a cost," she said.

"Jarl Beinersson drinks in Valhalla tonight with our fallen brothers and sisters. They feast with the gods," declared Ubbe.

"We must honour our brothers and sisters and ensure their safe passage to Valhalla," agreed Brenna.

"And tonight," Ubbe turned to face the great hall. "We feast!"

Cheers of joy and victory echoed through the hall. Platters of food were carried in by slaves, including the roasted pig sacrificed to the gods as thanks for their victory. Beer flowed freely.

Ubbe turned back to her, admiration reflected in his eyes. "And drink to Brenna, the Valkyrie of Birca. Skal!"

She let the shouts of victory wash over her. For tonight, she was still the Fru of Birca.

6

The longboat pulled alongside the dock at Fornsigtuna with little fanfare, lost amongst the urgent activity. It was mid-afternoon and the breeze off the water kept the early autumn heat from causing discomfort. Vali stepped ashore, his curious eyes watching as shields, axes and swords were distributed to leather-clad warriors.

"Well met, Gunnar," he greeted the huscarl striding toward him.

"Well met, Vali. I trust your voyage was blessed by the gods."

"Ja, Freyr blessed us with prosperity and good weather. Tell me, Gunnar," Vali gestured around him. "What is happening here?"

Gunnar motioned for Vali and his crew to follow him. "Sigurd the Black attacked Birca before the sun rose this morning."

Pulse quickening, Vali clenched his fists to keep his alarm at bay. This was exactly the kind of attack he knew came for those who did not enforce their right to title.

"The town fell?"

"Nei, Birca holds," said Gunnar, guiding them through the waiting warriors and bustling villagers preparing food and equipment for their army. "They suffered heavy losses."

He paused to look Vali in the eye. "Jarl Beinersson among them."

The back and forth of the town faded, blood thundering between his ears. Swallowing hard to force the moisture to his mouth and form the words he needed to say. "What of Brenna?"

"She lives." Gunnar regarded him with suspicious eyes. Their relationship had been common knowledge before her marriage to the jarl.

Relief jolted his body into motion. The hurried tasks of those around him returned to Vali's consciousness.

"They are calling her Valkyrie. Her prowess on the battlefield prevented Sigurd and his men from prevailing."

"She is a fine shieldmaiden," agreed Vali as relief surged through him. "What of Sigurd? Why did he not claim the jarldom?"

"It seems he did not know Tarben had fallen in battle," Gunnar shrugged. "More likely he was too busy saving his hide from Brenna's wrath. Aric is preparing to travel to Birca to reinforce their defences."

They reached the great hall, where two huscarls stood aside to allow them to enter. The hall was empty save the men sitting around the King's table and the servants who waited on them. A fire lit in the oblong pit running through the centre of the floor warmed the room.

"Vali," King Aric rose from the table of nobles and warriors. "The gods continue to favour my kingdom by returning you to our shores this day."

He forced down his lingering resentment of the King and his decision to offer Brenna's hand in marriage to someone else, despite knowing what existed between the two of them. He bowed his head in deference as he spoke.

"King Aric, I am sorry to hear Sigurd still troubles your lands."

Aric clapped his shoulder. "Ja, it is time we rid ourselves of this man once and for all. But come, you must be hungry." He ordered the servants to bring food and beer for Vali, and his crew who settled on another table.

"Join us, Vali," he motioned for him to sit with them. "I would be most grateful for your sword in the battle to come."

Vali moved towards the table. Aric offering an olive branch was a clear indication he needed more men in the impending battle.

Room was made and food and beer placed in front of him. He nodded across the table at Ragnar, the King's chief huscarl. "Word of your daughter's triumph greeted my arrival, Ragnar. She does you proud."

The older man acknowledged his words, his steely blue eyes giving nothing away. Vali refused to let Ragnar unnerve him. The man wielded his battle axe with deadly precision and had threatened to use it on him if he stood in the way of Brenna's marriage.

"I have sent one hundred warriors over land to Birca," began Aric. "I plan to set sail with two long boats on the evening tide. Vali, will you and your men join us?"

All eyes turned to him. He swallowed the food in his mouth, washing it down with a swig of beer. "Of course. But what of your defences here? Does it not concern you that Sigurd may attack Fornsigtuna?" He motioned for the servant to refill his horn.

"Or he may send forces to both," said Ragnar. "Which is why we are preparing for attack both here and in Birca."

"Why don't we attack Sigurd on his own lands?" asked Gunnar, leaning across the long, wooden table. "We know he lost many warriors in his defeat today."

"Ja, it is true," said Aric. "But he left Birca without claiming it for himself. I cannot be sure he did not know Tarben was dead and planned on taking Fornsigtuna, and potentially Uppsala, as a bigger prize."

"Surely Sigurd would not think himself so exceptional as to disturb the great temple?" asked Vali. The temple of Uppsala was the epicentre of their beliefs; a festival was held there every nine years, where sacrifices were offered to the gods for the people's ongoing protection and prosperity.

"Who knows what is in the mind of Sigurd," snarled Aric. "The priests have been warned and warriors sent to defend the temple if it comes to it."

"Sigurd knows the King will travel to Birca to install a new jarl," said Ragnar.

Vali's brow lifted in surprise. "Your daughter has not inherited the jarldom from her husband?"

"Nei, the jarl of such an important stronghold will be determined by the King." His disdain was barely disguised. "Besides, Brenna has seen only twenty summers. She knows naught about the ruling of men and territory."

The discussion of strategy continued around him. Vali kept his eyes on his food, contemplating Ragnar's assessment of both himself, and his daughter. Brenna agreed to marry Jarl Beinersson because she wanted to rule Birca by his side. Brenna had made her choice and left him without a backward glance. He did not imagine her ambitions would have died with her husband, even if her father judged her not yet ready to rule.

Of greater consternation was the apparent scorn with which Ragnar regarded him. Did he think now Brenna was free he would once again try to persuade her to join him on the open seas? He knew his daughter naught if he thought she was not scheming for her position as Fru of Birca to be retained.

The men around the table reached agreement on their plans. The King raised his horn. "Skal!"

"Skal!"

Vali drained the horn and stood. He had spent enough time in the company of the King.

"I imagine they will want some time with their women-folk before setting sail," said Gunnar with a wink, inclining his head towards Vali's crew.

Vali nodded. Turning on his heel he headed tover to his men.

"We sail to Birca on the evening tide."

"I thought as much," said Frode.

"Go be with your women and families. We'll meet at the docks two hours before the tide."

AFTER LEAVING THE HALL, Vali walked through the market-place, taking the path leading past the trading tables and the animal enclosures, towards the smaller structures closer to the mountains. As a child, Vali had lived in one of the longhouses with his parents and two sisters, and three other families. The men had all sailed with his father. When they went to sea, the wives and children were left to look out for each other until the men returned.

"Vali," his father would say each time he left to go raid-ing. "You are the man of the house now. You mind your mother and look after your sisters. I expect you to keep them safe when I am not here."

His father had taught him to fight and he'd practised

long and hard with Brenna when his father was away. While he'd worshipped his sire and couldn't wait to join him out at sea, he revelled in the knowledge his father trusted him to keep his family safe in his absence.

When he was killed, Vali had no choice but to take care of his family. As soon as he was able, he joined a raiding party.

He'd soon discovered his mother, Eira was expected to serve the other families if she wished to remain in the long-house, Vali moved her and his sisters to a smaller hut on the outskirts of Fornsigtuna. Eira's other choice had been to marry again, a choice she felt was not in the best interests of her daughters, whose fate would rest in the decisions of a man that did not care for them as their own father would. Vali respected the choice, and the sacrifice his mother had been prepared to make.

The light brown plait fell over the shoulder of his youngest sister, Tove, as she tended the garden at the front of the hut. Chickens pecked at the ground beside her.

"Those birds will eat all your crops if you leave them out," he said.

"Vali," Tove exclaimed, jumping to her feet. "You're home."

The girl ran into his arms and he noted that her head rested under his chin now.

"You've grown taller."

"And older."

"Ja, that's right." He kept his arm around her shoulder as they headed toward the hut.

"Did you bring me a present?" Her blue eyes shone with hope.

"Hmmm, let me see." Vali reached into the pouch tied to

his belt, withdrawing a pendant of blue gems tied with a ribbon for her neck.

"Vali, it's beautiful," she took the gift in her hands. "Where did you get it?"

"From a little town in Francia. It reminded me of your eyes."

"Vali?" His mother appeared in the doorway of the hut. "Oh thank the gods, you're home safe again."

He accepted her embrace, breathing in her familiar scent of fresh pine and wild flowers. Vali let the comfort of home strip away his lack of sleep and the tension of his meeting with Aric. His passion may be the sea, but his heart felt whole when he was surrounded by the ones he loved the most. Well, most of the ones he loved.

"Come in and let me look at you." Eira turned his face from side to side, assuring herself he was in one piece. "As handsome as ever," she whispered.

He leant his forehead against his mother's, letting her words soothe the cracks that still existed in his heart.

A tiny cry captured his attention. Turning, he spied his other sister at the table.

"Vali, come and meet your nephew." Siri rose from the bench she'd been sitting on, the bundle in her arms making himself known.

"You have a son?" He smiled, his delight mirroring the look on his sister's face.

"Ja, a son."

She shifted the baby into the crook of his arm. "We named him Vali."

His breath caught as he looked at the tiny boy in wonder. "Vali?"

"You were our protector and our provider when Father died. Without you, only the gods know where we might have ended up. We want our child to grow to be as loyal and brave as you."

He kept his gaze on the baby in his arms, allowing only his namesake to see the emotion welling behind his eyes. His sister's words touched him deep inside. He'd always seen his role as a duty, one bound in love and honour, rather than reproach.

Siri took her son from his arms and they settled around the table.

"You've heard the news of Birca?" asked Eira.

"Ja, the King has asked us to sail with him on the evening's tide."

"But you've only just come home," pouted Tove. "Can't the King can send someone else?" She stood and stalked around the table, busying herself at the fire pit.

"Nei, child," said Eira. "Your brother is one of his best warriors. Of course, Aric wants Vali by his side."

"Anyone would think you missed me, sister?"

"Mayhap I'm tired of doing your chores as well as mine."

"Tove is still angry that you did not fight harder for Brenna," said Siri. "And now she lives too far away for Tove to follow her around like a puppy at her heels."

Steel pins pricked at his heart. His sister thought he was to blame for Brenna leaving?

"Hush now." Eira's tone brooked no further argument. "Brenna's marriage was the decision of the King. There was naught for Vali to do but accept it."

Eira rose and picked up a wicker basket, holding it out at her daughter. "Tove, gather some more vegetables from the garden."

Turning to her son, she softened her voice. "Let me make you a decent meal before you leave, ja?"

He gave his mother a grateful smile, although it failed to reach his eyes.

They ate and talked. His sisters sharing the news of home and Vali describing the sights and treasures he'd found. Siri's husband, Hagen, returned and he spoke of the preparations being made to defend Fornsigtuna should the need arise. His mother and Tove would join Siri and the baby at their farm if Sigurd attacked.

As the sun began its slow descent, Vali stood to take his leave.

"May the gods keep you safe, my son," his mother said, releasing him from her embrace. She looked him in the eye. "And however you find Brenna, be kind."

Emotions warred within him. Tove had succeeded in opening the wounds that had barely crusted over. He knew she missed Brenna but it was not he who was responsible for her pain - or his. He returned his mother's steady gaze. He did not consider Brenna worthy of his kindness.

7

*B*renna stood on the dock alongside Ubbe and the rest of the council. The sun was beginning to set, taking the warmth of the day with it. The breeze had picked up, helping King Aric's boats cross the final stretch of water. His land soldiers had arrived on foot and were finding refreshment in the great hall.

She was pleased the King had responded swiftly to her request for help, yet her anxiety over what was to become of her raged an internal war she hoped was not obvious. Squeezing her fingernails into the palms of her clenched fists, she kept her chin held high.

Brenna may have the support of Birca's noblemen, but it would count for naught if the King wished her to return to her father's home. Being without child for six full moons would be perceived as her fault, regardless of Tarben's lack of heirs from any of the other women he'd bedded in his lifetime. Still, she feared no man of position would want her in his marriage bed and risk his own lineage.

What would she do if Aric allowed her to stay in Birca? The King required an experienced statesman to oversee the gateway to the Baltic trade routes, and with only twenty summers under her belt she knew he would never consider her to take over from Tarben. Her youth would also attract the interest of too many others, like Sigurd, who thought they could wrest the jarldom from her by force.

The thought of countless more deaths in the defence of Birca because of an inexperienced jarl set her heart beating in panic. Of course she could fight. That was the one thing she did better than most. But other than her skills as a shieldmaiden, how would she support herself in Birca, alone?

The King's longboat reached the dock. He stepped aboard, rich furs trailing behind him. Aric was shorter than most men but made up for it with his broad shoulders and enormous presence. He cropped his blonde hair close to his scalp, revealing the tattoos that symbolised his power and wisdom. He wore his beard long and his ice blue eyes missed naught.

Brenna bowed low, along with the others waiting on the dock.

"Rise," said the King, striding toward them. "Brenna, Ubbe, I am heartened to see you both alive."

"King Aric, it is with regret such matters have brought you to Birca," responded Ubbe, accepting the embrace of his King.

"Indeed."

He turned his attention to Brenna with a tight smile and distant eyes that gave nothing away. She inhaled a steadying breath, determined not to appear weak despite her internal panic.

"Your valour in battle has been well-described. The wanderers will surely tell the tale of Birca's Valkyrie."

"Our victory was fated by the gods," she replied.

"As it seems was the death of your husband," said the King, lowering his voice.

Brenna inclined her head in deference to Tarben, and to hide the panic she felt spike inside her. She mourned the Jarl's passing but knew in her heart she mourned it more for the loss of her own position.

"We have waited for you to arrive before performing the funeral ritual."

Aric nodded. "I will preside over the ritual once we have refreshed from our journey."

"Come," said Ubbe, who'd been standing patiently at her side. "Your men await you in the great hall."

As the King and his entourage started towards the hall, Brenna waited to greet her father as warriors came ashore, bringing weapons and provisions for their stay. She had not seen either of her parents since her wedding feast and she was keen to feel her father's warm embrace.

"Well met, Daughter," Ragnar stood before her.

"Well met, Father," she held her breath, hoping he could spare a few moments from his duties as huscarl for her.

He kissed her on either cheek before folding her into his strong arms. She inhaled his familiar scent of leather and fire smoke, and the tension she'd been holding since the day she'd arrived in Birca started to uncoil. "You are well, Daughter?"

"I am," she smiled up at him relishing that for once, she was not alone. "How is Mother?"

"Your mother is well. She prays to Freya every night for your health and happiness."

Brenna's smile grew wider. She missed her mother, Hertha, and her wise counsel more than words. If she were to return to Fornsigtuna, she could look forward to seeing her mother every day once more.

"Come, let us join the King," Ragnar tucked her arm inside his own. As she turned to walk away, a figure disembarking one of the longboats was illuminated in the torch light. His fluid motions were as familiar to her as her own face. Her breath caught in her throat as her feet turned to lead. The instant yearning for his touch set a fire galloping through her body.

"Why is he here?" she whispered.

Ragnar glanced in the direction of her stare. "Aric asked him to join us." His tone hardened. He tugged on her arm, forcing her to turn away.

Vali Hrolfsson was a complication she did not need. They had not parted on good terms and she could little imagine he would look sympathetically at her current situation. Straightening her spine, she allowed her father to lead her away, determined not to give Vali any further thought.

Unfortunately, her body, starved of a man's attention for too long, and her traitorous heart had other ideas.

THE CALM WATERS of the fjord were in stark contrast to his churning gut. Even from a distance Vali could make out the shape of Brenna standing on the dock. She stood tall, her blonde hair lifting and falling with the breeze. He could almost feel her soft locks against the backs of his hands as he held her face, Brenna sitting astride him with eyes full of lust. His every instinct was to leap ashore and go to her, claim her as his own.

Instead, he cursed himself for the fool he was. She gave him away. It would serve him well to remember this during the time he would be forced to remain in her presence.

Brenna might be without a husband, yet she stood at the head of the town waiting to receive the King, every inch the

Fru of Birca. Blood boiled in his veins as he turned and readied himself to disembark. He imagined she was already positioning herself, despite Ragnar's proclamation that his daughter was too young to be jarl in her own right. Vali kept his eyes on the task of tethering the boat to the dock, barking orders at his men. He had no use for Brenna and her ambitions.

When the last of his warriors had alighted, Vali could find no more reason to linger. Gritting his teeth, he turned towards the village in time to see Brenna being led away on the arm of her father. She hadn't seen him. Or if she had, Brenna had not lowered herself to wait and acknowledge him.

"That suits me well," he muttered.

He was here at the request of Aric, and there was no purpose in seeking an audience with Brenna. He'd do well to remember that. Setting his shoulders, he marched forward to find his sleeping quarters for the time he would have to spend in Birca. Then he needed beer and food. Mayhap a woman to distract him from his memories.

8

The body of Jarl Beinersson lay in a small boat, draped in fine silks and furs with his sword and shield clasped to his chest. Around the body was silver and treasure, food and beer and the head of Tarben's horse, as was customary for a man of the Jarl's status. All to accompany him in his journey, and for his use in Valhalla.

The people of Birca had gathered along the mouth of the fjord to watch the funeral. Brenna listened as King Aric spoke the funeral rites. The wind picked up the water's cool fingers and swept them across her face with not enough force to wipe her tears away. Sadness sat across her shoulders, its mantle growing heavier with each passing moment. She lifted her chin and straightened her spine. It shamed her to admit her tears were not for Tarben, but for herself.

Her husband's death had placed her future in the hands of the gods, and of the King. In the gods, she trusted. Aric had arranged her marriage to Tarben and she had, with her mother's wise counsel in mind, relented. It suited her ambition, yet the price she'd paid for the marriage had been heavy. Vali.

His memory always haunted her, but nothing prepared her for seeing him again. It had taken all of her strength not to close the distance between them on the dock, to feel his arms around her. He'd always been her safe haven.

Instinctively, her eyes roamed the shoreline like a wolf in search of her mate. She was met with a stare so filled with loathing that she had to look away.

It was better this way. Better to remember Vali wanted the freedom of the seas and she'd convinced herself that marriage to Tarben was what she wanted. To be the adored wife of the Jarl of Birca. Only, adoration wasn't what she'd found.

In the beginning, Brenna wondered if Tarben's limp manhood and ensuing resentment of her was the gods cursing her for turning her back on Vali. Decreeing that she would never feel the touch of her husband - or any man - again. But she had always believed the gods had something more in store for her. The Seer had said so. Mayhap they were now righting the imbalance and clearing her path to return to the man she loved.

The torchbearers approached the boat. Within seconds the body of the fallen jarl was engulfed in flames as the boat was pushed into deeper waters. The breeze that had tormented Brenna turned its attention to carrying the warrior to his final destination in Valhalla.

Her tears stained her cheeks as she watched the boat drift across the fjord, away from the port. Villagers began to move away, then the warriors and council. Finally, the King and his guard withdrew, leaving Brenna alone. As her ties to this place slipped away, anxiety crept up her spine. Its icy tentacles creating a vice around her heart. The King had still given no indication of what his plans for her might be. That her fate was not in her own hands set her blood to simmering beneath the surface.

Approaching footsteps forced her to straighten her spine and shake off her discomposure. Turning, she expected to see the servant girl coming to fetch her in readiness for the evening's festivities. Instead, Vali stood before her.

"Well met, Brenna," he nodded briefly.

She quickly swallowed her surprise, careful to keep her face and tone neutral. "So formal, Vali."

"My condolences. Jarl Beinersson was a great warrior." He ignored her attempt to speak freely as they always had.

"Thank you, he was." Brenna could hear his angry undertones and resisted the urge to reach out and touch his arm. To ask him to put his anger aside.

"He feasts in Odin's Great Hall tonight."

"Ja," she agreed. Vali could barely look her in the eye. Her own anger wavered under the pain of his hostility.

From the corner of her eye, she spied the figure of her father and felt his gaze come to rest upon them. "Will you be joining the feast tonight?"

"My men and I will toast the Jarl, and you and your great victory." He turned on his heel and walked swiftly back to the village.

Brenna bowed her head in acknowledgement of his words, and what it cost her to hear the hate he carried in his heart.

9

*V*ali walked through the outskirts of the village, on his way to the great hall. In the distance he could see the silhouettes of men and women feasting on the lawns surrounding the hall. He could hear their roars of laughter and proclamations of victory and thanks to the gods. But here amongst the longhouses, women wept softly for their lost children and husbands. Siblings held each other as they cried for their mothers. Warriors moaned as the healers tended to their wounds. The other side of victory huddled within pain and grief, away from the celebration. This was a side he knew existed but tried hard to avoid, as did most of the Vikings he fought with. It reminded him of his father and the pain his death brought upon his family. Victory or Valhalla; that is all he wanted to think about.

He noticed a small procession coming from the back of the great hall. Slaves bearing food and beer wove in and out of longhouses and fireside vigils, making sure no one went hungry.

"May the gods bless and keep the Valkyrie of Birca," he

heard one woman say as she shared the bread and meat amongst those around her. A whisper of warmth stroked his heart.

First, she saves them, then she feeds them.

As he approached the hall, the heavy sadness of the dark night retreated behind the glory of victory. Beer flowed freely both outside and within the great hall, with most of the revellers drinking their fill during the time he'd taken to gather himself after speaking with Brenna. It was his duty to offer his condolences, despite the risk of choking on his anger.

His crew had secured a table near the entrance of the hall. A drinking horn was placed in his hand as the men shuffled to make room for their Styrimaðr.

"Skal," he raised his horn before swallowing its contents in one gulp. His men were enjoying themselves, as well they should. Vali was conscious that they had barely stood on their homeland before being called into service again. They deserved to feast and drink with their King.

Vali helped himself to the roasted chicken and allowed his horn to be filled to the brim once more. While the townspeople celebrated their great victory over Sigurd the Black, Vali and his crew relived their own tales of plunder and wealth from their recent raids.

Letting the exaggerated tales of honour and renown unfold around him, Vali let his eyes wander to the front of the hall where Brenna sat on the King's table as the honoured widow and victorious shieldmaiden. Men leant in and over her, their own stories from the battle-field competing for prominence. Brenna sat amongst them, her thin-lipped smile not reaching her eyes. Beer spilt from horns and spittle flew as voices grew louder and more animated. She did not join the banter, nor was she included. The price of her ambition.

Her chin remained raised and her back straight in what appeared a well-practised stance. Her eyes searched for no one in the crowd. She was a beautiful accessory, although one nobody laid any claim too. Even her father paid her no mind as he conversed with the King.

Vali ignored the desire coursing through his body, pushing away all thoughts of taking her hand and disappearing into the night with her. Despite her ambitions, she was not a ruler and her place was not amongst the noblemen of Birca. He welcomed the sense of spiteful providence that settled in his belly as proof his heart no longer pined for her.

BRENNA TOOK her opportunity to leave the feast when the two men talking at each other above her head became distracted by one of the slave girls clearing the table. Standing, she made her way to where the King sat in deep conversation with her father.

"King Aric, Father," she spoke when they turned their attention to her. "I'm afraid the past few days have taken their toll and I long for sleep."

"Of course, Brenna," King Aric rose from his chair. "Although I don't know how restful your sleep will be."

He gestured to the bedchamber behind the wall where they stood. It was true, the noise of the feast would keep her awake. However, Brenna knew the King's motivation was not concern for her rest.

"I asked my servant to find appropriate quarters, sire. I have need of only a bed to lay my head upon. I thought you might prefer to use these rooms during your stay."

"Very thoughtful," he nodded his thanks. "Sleep well."

"Daughter, I will accompany you to your quarters."

Brenna gratefully accepted the arm Ragnar offered.

They wove their way through the crowd, men raising their drinking horns to her as she passed, cheering loudly their thanks to the gods for the fall of Sigurd. Brenna acknowledged them with nods of thanks, barely flinching as beer spilt over her from their horns. She knew they drank to their victory, and to forget their losses. Ragnar remained silent; an unusual occurrence for her father. Unease wrapped itself around her shoulders. Did he have news that she would not welcome?

The cool night air was a relief from the overcrowded hall. As they approached the longhouse where Gita had arranged a place for Brenna to sleep, she found herself surrounded by half a dozen townspeople. One by one, they gripped her arm and murmured their thanks for her protection and the provisions she'd sent. It pained her that she didn't know all of their names. As the Fru of Birca she'd not been embraced by the people, nor had Tarben encouraged it.

Her first opportunity to do something for her adopted home had been amidst bloodshed and fear. She wondered how long her actions would live in the memories of these people if she was suddenly forced to make her home with them without the protection of a husband or family?

Gita waited for them at the door of the longhouse.

"Leave us," said Ragnar as they approached.

Brenna turned to her father, sensing her fate was about to be revealed to her.

"You have done well by these people, Brenna. You fought for them when called to do so."

"Of course," she replied.

"Brenna, I must ask this." Ragnar lowered his voice. "Is there any chance you are with child?"

She swallowed the lump of indignation that rose, not at the question, but at the memory of her loveless marriage. She shook her head.

"You're sure."

She looked her father in the eye. "I am."

He held her stare momentarily before giving a light nod of acceptance. "The King sails for Fornsigtuna in two days. You will accompany us on the journey and return home."

Relief washed over her, easing the knot in her shoulders even more. She would not be left to make her own way in Birca.

"Ja, Father." In two days she would see her mother again. That thought alone had her heart filling with joy.

Her father bid her good night and as she watched him return to the hall, she caught sight of another group of villagers watching her with grateful intent.

Disappointment stirred deep within. This was why she wanted to rule; to ensure everyone received protection and care. To make sure the sacrifices of some did not become a burden for their families. Brenna hoped the new jarl would consider the lives of all his people important, not just those of his council, warriors and traders.

10

*T*he evening's feast was a distant memory as the town returned to normal. Traders haggled over prices with merchants; farmers displayed their produce. Women and children focused on their chores while preparations for fortifying the town's defences were well-underway.

Vali was not required at the great hall with the King and Birca's council. He and his crew were on hand to fight if necessary, not to participate in the decisions and strategies of war. He'd left his men tending to the longboat and their weapons while he went in search of the forge to get a new handle for his axe.

The forge was a hive of activity with villagers wanting to replace broken spears and lost axes. Vali almost didn't notice the woman sitting off to the side, sharpening her axe with a whetstone. Without her finery, wearing a plain overdress, Brenna looked like a farmer's wife maintaining her tools. But Brenna was the one person Vali could never ignore, no matter how much he wanted to. And the axe she was sharpening was no farmer's tool.

"Your presence is not required in the great hall?"

Brenna's steady stroke of the whetstone against the blade slowed for just a second. Pursing her lips, she held the blade up to inspect her work.

"Neither is yours, it seems." She turned the axe over and started sharpening the other side.

"They've no need for the thoughts of a lowly Styrimaðr of a raiding party."

Brenna grunted.

"Nor the likes of the Valkyrie of Birca?" He stepped closer, pretending to take a closer look at the axe she was sharpening. He wasn't sure where he was going with this conversation but Vali felt as though he'd stepped back in time. Brenna looked like her old self, her mind focused on the task at hand. He could almost forget the anger that still burned inside him.

"The Valkyrie of Birca is returning to Fornsigtuna on tomorrow's tide." Her rhythmic strokes of the stone remained constant.

"You're coming home?" Vali knew the King planned on installing a new jarl as soon as possible, but he'd never considered that Brenna would return to Fornsigtuna. A spark of hope flickered deep inside.

She glanced up from her work. "Ja."

Vali placed a hand on hers to still the movement. He heard the subtle hiss of her breath catching.

"What will you do?"

Her blue eyes stared up into his and he felt his anger slip away.

She raised her shoulders, then let them fall. "I don't know."

His heart hammered against his chest as he stepped closer. Brenna held his gaze. He sent a silent prayer to Freya that he wasn't imagining the longing he saw in her eyes. A longing that mirrored his own. Brenna's hands fell to her sides, removing the barrier between them. He raised his hand, tracing a finger along her jaw. The noise and heat of the forge disappeared, replaced by the beating of his heart and the sound of his own breath as he leaned closer.

The rider was almost upon them before Vali noticed the shift in attention of the people around them. They both stepped back as the moment shattered beneath the hooves of the horse rearing on its hind legs.

"An army approaches," shouted the scout. "They carry the flag of Sigurd the Black".

Vali looked at Brenna as fear erupted around them.

"I have to go." She gathered her weapons and headed towards the longhouses.

Vali stared after her for only a second before breaking into a run towards the docks.

BRENNA RAN FOR THE LONGHOUSE, her skirts bunched at her side. The scout had said Sigurd's army was less than half a day's march away over land. Would they attack by sea as well? No boats had been sighted. Perhaps they'd landed further down the coast and would attack from either side? She needed to get to the great hall to hear how the King would defend the town.

As she reached the rows of longhouses behind the markets, she was swarmed with children.

"Fru Brenna, is it true? Has Sigurd returned?"

"Has he come back to kill us all?"

Frightened eyes surrounded her.

"Will you stop him again?"

"Please help us."

Dropping her weapons at her feet, she knelt before the children. She took the hand of the smallest child, a girl of five years or so, oi her own.

"Last time Sigurd came, we were all asleep in our beds. We had no time to prepare." She noticed more children and some adults joined the group. "But this time the gods have warned us that Sigurd is coming. We have time to prepare."

She gave the children a reassuring smile. "And you have time to hide. Gather your families and your neighbours and go into the mountains."

Brenna rose and addressed the adults. "Hurry, you have time to get to safety. Take the children and those that cannot fight to the caves in the mountains. Arm yourselves with whatever you can carry."

"Do you think he'll find us in the mountains," said the little girl.

"Nei. I'll ask Heimdall to watch over you."

"And we'll pray to the Allfather for your victory, Valkyrie," came the response from a voice in the crowd.

Brenna nodded. "Those of you who can fight, get your weapons and make your way to the marketplace. The rest of you, hide in the mountains."

Gita waited for her at the longhouse.

"I've laid out your trousers and tunic."

"And my chest armour?"

"Ja, it's all here."

Brenna pulled the overdress over her head and quickly dressed in her battle clothes. As Gita came to help her tighten the leather strapping on her corset, she noticed the girl's hands shaking.

"Gita, you need to concentrate. Pull the strapping tighter."

"I'm sorry, Fru." Her face was flushed. "I'm afraid Sigurd has brought more men this time."

"And so have we. The King brought his own army to defend Birca."

"Will it be enough?"

Brenna fastened the dagger to the belt around her waist and reached for her sword to sheath. "It has to be enough." Strapping the shield to her arm, she picked up her spear and her newly sharpened axe. "Get to the mountains, take any stragglers with you."

"Ja, Fru." Gita hurried away.

Brenna took a breath and acknowledged the rapid beating of her heart against her chest and the stone of fear that was lodged in her belly. Closing her eyes, she prayed.

"Allfather, make me fast and accurate, let my blade strike true and my arm be swifter than any who seek to destroy me. Odin, grant us victory this day."

Banging her axe against her shield, she set off for the great hall. The rows between the longhouses were all but deserted with only a few remaining mothers chasing their children or farmers collecting their weapons. As she drew closer to the marketplace, the numbers increased tenfold.

Forcing her way through the crowd to the great hall, she exhaled with relief when the huscarl let her straight through to the King.

"Brenna, you will fight with us."

"Ja, what is your plan, sire?"

"We will march out to meet Sigurd outside of the village walls," Aric said as servants pulled his chainmail into place and strapped the leather cuffs to his forearms. "We will leave a guard inside the walls to watch for any attack by sea."

A guard? Half a dozen men? It is not enough. "And what of the eastern flank?"

Every head in the hall turned to look at her. The King's eyes hardened and she forced herself to breathe. Aric was not a king that welcomed an opinion which differed to his once his mind was made up.

"What of it?" asked Ragnar, stepping forward.

"When Sigurd was defeated, his longboats sailed towards the east." She kept her voice steady, knowing the lives of her people depended on the King and Ragnar hearing her.

"We've seen no boats in the fjord and we are leaving a guard at the dock in case they return," replied her father.

"Ja, but what if the boats made land further along the coast? They attacked on two fronts last time after landing. Do you think they'd again adopt a similar strategy?"

Her father was a gifted strategist in battle, she had to make him understand.

"Sigurd has given us plenty of warning that his army approaches from the west," said Ubbe. He moved closer to the conversation from where he'd been watching from the side. "Mayhap they are hoping we send all our warriors out to meet them, leaving the village and the docks unprotected."

"Send a scout to investigate." Aric pulled at the leather cuffs, ensuring they were secure.

"There's no time," said Ragnar. "We must decide now if we divide our forces to fight on two fronts."

All eyes returned to King Aric. He stared hard at Brenna, as if the truth of her claim would be revealed under his scrutiny. Brenna stood firm, despite her thundering heart, and the King shifted his stare to Ubbe, who had come to stand by her side.

"Brenna and Ubbe, you will take warriors from the village and march out to the east." His voice carried a clear warning. The responsibility for this decision would rest with her.

Relief gave her renewed strength. She knew in her gut she was right. Rolling her shoulders back, she banged her axe against her shield and left to find her warriors.

11

*V*ali saw Brenna leave the hall, deep in conversation with the warrior Ubbe as they headed towards the marketplace. Groups of men and women, armed and ready, waited for their instructions. The huscarl and the King's army stood at attention as Ragnar strode towards them. He barked his orders and they moved off in the direction of the approaching army.

He noticed the natives of Birca stayed behind. Ubbe and Brenna stood side by side and addressed the remaining soldiers.

"Vali, the King has marched out," said Frode. "We need to move."

Behind him, his men stood at the ready.

"Just a minute," he said, moving in the direction of Brenna and ignoring Frode's frustration.

Pushing his way through the crowd, he reached out and took hold of Brenna's arm to get her attention. "What is happening? The King has marched out?"

"We are preparing to defend an attack from the east."

"More of Sigurd's army has been spotted?"

"Nei." She turned to face him. "His boats escaped to the east after the last attack. I believe they have landed further along the coast and hope to catch us without any defences in the village. Ubbe and I are leading a force to meet them."

His heart and head reacted as one, not doubting her battle instincts and needing to be near her. "I'll join you."

Her eyes searched his face. "Your crew is here at the request of the King."

He nodded. "I'm here to fight, to defend Birca." He squared his shoulders, daring her to dismiss him.

"Alright. Your sword is most welcome."

Something skin to pride prickled his scalp. Returning to his men, Vali explained the division of forces.

"So, we are chasing ghosts?" asked Frode.

"We're following orders," said Vali, his anger flaring.

"We're here to fight and the enemy approaches in the opposite direction," growled Frode.

"The King agreed to split the defences across both fronts," Vali drew himself up to his full height and stepped closer to Frode. "Are you disagreeing with the King's decision?"

The other man's face screwed up in a protest he refrained from giving voice to. Turning, he picked up his shield and axe then stepped back into the ranks of the crew. Vali glared at his men, shutting down any further challenges to his authority.

"Let's go."

VALI and his men marched out behind the warriors of Birca. As they cleared the last of the longhouses and moved through the farming land, he could see Brenna out in front and he resisted the urge to move forward and join her. He needed to focus. Brenna could handle herself in battle. Worrying about her would likely get him killed.

They started to climb the summit when the group was halted in its tracks. Word came back that the enemy was advancing up the other side of the hill.

Vali glanced sideways at Frode. "It seems the ghosts are flesh and blood."

Frode smirked. "Don't worry brother, as long as I get to fight, I am happy."

Ubbe and Brenna spread the warriors along the ridge. Behind them, archers readied themselves for the first wave of attack. Vali lost sight of Brenna as she moved further along the line.

"Odin, grant us victory," he murmured as the rush of the impending fight lit a fire in his belly.

Sigurd's army was oblivious to the warriors waiting for them on the mountaintop. Vali could hear their footfall getting heavier as they neared. Another minute stretched in silent anticipation. His heart rate picked up its pace in readiness for battle.

"Loose!" came the command and arrows rained down on the unsuspecting warriors.

The battle cry of Birca echoed into the valley below.

"Forward!"

The army moved forward as Sigurd's men scrambled to regroup. The opposing force was smaller than Birca's warriors; clearly the survivors of the first attack on the town; and they weren't expecting Birca to anticipate this attack.

"Shield wall!"

Vali and his crew stood shoulder to shoulder with their shields overlapping. Behind them, the farmers and merchants stood with their makeshift weapons. In the front line, they raised their spears and prepared to attack.

The battle cry went up again and the fight began in earnest. Vali thrust his spear between the enemy's shields, finding flesh on more than one occasion. As Sigurd's defences crumbled, Vali withdrew his shield and swung his sword at the nearest warrior.

He hacked and chopped, rarely needing his shield to deflect the blows aimed at him. The bloodlust took hold and he relished the chance to bring the enemy to its knees. Beside him, his crew fought viscously, giving no mercy to those in their path.

Barely an hour had passed when Sigurd's men retreated. Vali and his crew gave chase, taking out a dozen more Vikings before leaving the rest to run for safety. Ubbe met them as they made their way back up the hill.

"We've sent two dozen men to Aric. Sigurd sent a much bigger army to attack from the west."

"Do you want us to follow?" asked Vali.

"Nei, we need you to guard the east in case they return. We have mostly farmers and traders left. We'll need your swords if the fight comes back."

Vali nodded his assent and set up look outs along the summit, ordering the rest of the soldiers to rest and tend to the wounded.

"What's the damage?" he asked Frode.

Frode grinned. "Not even a scratch," he said referring to the crew. "So, your Valkyrie was right."

"She has her father's instincts for battle." He'd not seen Brenna since they'd spied Sigurd's army. He scanned the groups of warriors left to defend against any further attacks.

"Brenna went to the western front." Frode answered his unspoken question.

Vali grunted. She was alive.

"Send a scout in each direction. Have them report back to me."

Frode nodded and went to find two scouts.

Vali gave a silent prayer of thanks to the gods for delivering them safely from the fight. He hoped the King's army would soon prevail in the west.

Then he could go home to Fornsigtuna. And Brenna.

12

The battle was evenly matched when Brenna and her reinforcements met up with King Aric atop the ridge on the outskirts of Birca. The fight had turned to hand to hand combat and the ground beneath the warriors was muddy with blood and sweat. The dead lay where they fell while the wounded tried to crawl out of the mire. Brenna took all of this in without allowing it to mean anything. Death was part of life, even more so on the battle-field. If Sigurd meant to take Birca then she would defend the town and its people with everything she had.

Riding on the high of defeating the intruders coming from the east, their arrival quickly turned the advantage to Birca. Brenna swung her axe as an extension of herself, aiming low at the legs before targeting the arms and torso. The swing and pivot was a bloody dance, and she warmed to a fight with warriors who were fresher than the depleted force she'd faced earlier. Adrenalin kept the ache from her arms until the call of retreat finally sounded from Sigurd's men.

"Daughter!"

She turned towards her father's voice. Mud and blood stained every part of Ragnar.

"I see you've added another scar to your collection, Father." Blood flowed freely from the slice above his right eye.

"A scratch." He dismissed the wound. "What of the east? Was it as you expected?"

She nodded. "Ja, they sent the survivors from the last battle. It was hardly a fair fight."

"But they'd have strength enough to burn the town to the ground if they'd made it to Birca."

"Thank the gods they didn't."

Ragnar eyed his daughter thoughtfully. "You've lost naught of your skill and instinct."

Her father was a great warrior, renowned throughout the land, and his praise warmed her heart. She bowed her head in acknowledgment.

"Come, we must inform the King."

"Father, the villagers still hide in the mountains behind the town. I would let them know it's safe to return?"

Ragnar nodded once in agreement before heading towards the King.

Retrieving her axe from the neck of a dead warrior, she wiped the blade on his tunic. She could have sent a messenger to the mountains, but she felt a sense of duty to ensure they had remained safe, and to return them to the village. Her arms had begun to throb and fatigue would find her soon enough, so she set a fast pace towards the caves.

Within the hour she'd arrived to find the townspeople safe and well. Gita pushed her way forward to her mistress.

"Fru! Is it true? Sigurd is defeated?"

"Ja, Gita," she smiled. "We are victorious once more."

"Surely, Sigurd will not come back?"

Brenna took a deep breath and considered the servant girl, her eyes shining with hope. "Who knows the hearts and minds of greedy men, Gita. We can only pray to the gods that Sigurd has lost too many warriors to think of facing King Aric and his army any time soon."

"I prayed to the Allfather that you would lead us to victory," said Gita. "We all did."

Those around them nodded. "The Valkyrie of Birca has saved us again."

Brenna swallowed the lump that formed in her throat. Hot tears pricked the back of her eyes and threatened to spill, revealing her exhaustion and pride.

"Come," she started towards the village. "Let us return to help the wounded and feast the victory."

THE CELEBRATIONS WERE in full swing as warriors regaled each other with tales of their heroism over horns filled with beer. As she approached, men stopped to greet her - not out of deference to her position as the Jarl's widow, but as a warrior. They clapped their hands on her back and offered her refreshment. Some even started recounting their observations of Brenna's prowess with her axe. Those who fought with her on the eastern side spoke of her leadership and battle instincts.

Despite the stiffness setting into her limbs, she felt at ease amongst the people of Birca for the very first time. She'd fought with them, and for them. They accepted her as one of their own. Gladly, she accepted a horn filled with beer and joined in the story-telling and good-natured ribbing.

Aware that her weapons needed tending to, she excused herself and made her way to the longhouse. The short walk took three times as long as she was stopped along the way by children and villagers who wanted to thank her and tell her the stories they'd heard of her feats in battle. The mood was lighter this time, with less deaths and casualties amongst their own soldiers. She knew the bodies were being collected and pyres being built for the fallen to send them on their way to Valhalla. There would be sadness, but also rejoicing.

At the longhouse, Gita took her weapons, promising to clean them thoroughly. A bath had been drawn for her and Brenna sank gratefully into its warm depths. A long scratch she'd not noticed glistened on her left forearm. Her cheek and jaw were bruised. Minor ailments for such a bloody battle.

Adrenalin had carried her through the fighting, and now her own sense of pride was pulling her back to her fellow warriors to feast their victory. No more solitary meals in a hall full of conversations that she was never invited into. No more insincere smiles for a husband who cared naught for her. She had no need for her place at the King's table. Tonight, she would feast with the people.

VALI HEARD her laugh but could not see her amongst the King's men and warriors. Eventually his eyes fell upon Brenna's golden hair, sitting across the hall amongst a group of farmers turned soldiers in defence of their homes. He watched her eat and drink, talk and laugh; the way she'd always done when she'd lived in Fornsigtuna. She was so far removed from the Brenna who'd sat stiffly at King Aric's table the previous evening. She may want to rule, but Vali saw in her the spirit of a fierce shieldmaiden. She had more than earned the title of Valkyrie in her recent battles.

He made his way across the hall, resting his hand on her shoulder once he reached her table.

"Do my eyes deceive me? The Valkyrie of Birca is a mortal woman?"

"Nei," cried her table companions. "Brenna *is* Valkyrie, a true warrior."

Brenna laughed and they drank to their victory and to the fallen who feasted in the halls of Valhalla.

"Can I steal you away?" Vali whispered in her ear, lingering long enough to inhale her scent.

She turned to face him and he saw longing burning in her eyes. She nodded once and took her leave of her dinner companions. Once outside the hall, he reached and found her hand, moulding it into his own. As they got further from the outside celebrations, he pulled her close, wrapping his arm around her waist.

"Are you hurt?" he asked, tracing a finger along her bruised jaw.

"Nei," she whispered. "You?"

He shook his head.

"Mayhap I should see for myself that you are unharmed?"

Vali heard the slight tremor in her voice. He held her face between his hands and brought his forehead to rest against hers. "Ja, mayhap."

Taking her hand once more, he led her to his sleeping quarters. He'd been allocated one of the newly erected tents that housed the reinforcements Aric had brought with him. Inside, his furs made for a comfortable bed.

Finally alone with Brenna, nerves flipped inside his belly. It felt as if a lifetime had passed since he'd touched her. The beating of his heart drummed between his ears and his fingers trembled as they reached for her again. She ran her tongue over her lower lip, her eyes darkening with desire. Slowly he moved his mouth towards her, his lips brushing against hers.

Her breath was warm and sweet, her lips parting, asking him for more. He kissed her, slowly and gently. The taste of her turning his insides molten. He deepened the kiss, his tongue exploring her mouth. She responded in kind, pressing her body into his. His cock hardened and he fisted his hand in her hair, needing her to be closer still. Her moan caught between them.

Pulling back, he lifted his tunic, tugging it over his head. She stared at him in the muted moonlight, her eyes hungrily tracing his chest and abdomen. Sitting, he removed his boots before unlacing hers. Brenna loosened the tie of her overdress, letting it fall to her feet. Vali pushed his trousers down. They stood opposite each other, naked.

For a moment, he felt unsure. As if she read his mind, Brenna reached out and ran her hands across his chest, then slowly over his stomach. His cock stood at attention, eager to feel her touch. She cupped his balls and massaged his length. His nerves gave way to lust and he stilled her hands before he lost all control. Reaching for her braided hair, he pulled the tie free.

Vali laid her back against the furs, her golden locks fanning around her head. She watched him, the deep pools of her eyes drawing him in. Feathering kisses along her jawline, his hand found her breast, stroking the soft, fleshy underside. His lips brushed her hardened buds, her sighs encouraging him as his licked and sucked at each in turn. Her skin was soft under his calloused hands and eager lips. He paused at the bruising along her ribs, until she pushed his head down further, impatient for him to continue navigating the subtle curves and hidden troughs of her body.

A growl caught in his throat and he moved down to kiss her inner thighs as they fell open before him. She steered him closer to her sex, her fingers entangled in his hair. Her scent intoxicated him, pushing any other thought from his mind. Nuzzling against the soft curls, he took his time, aware of the effect he was having as her panting grew heavier and her fingers tightened against his skull.

He ran his tongue inside her slick folds and smiled as she moaned for more, pushing her wet and wanting mound against him. He blew softly against it, enjoying the torture he knew he was inflicting.

"Vali," she breathed.

Cupping his hands beneath her buttocks he pulled her closer.

"Ja," she whispered. "Please."

"As you wish," he growled before plunging his tongue inside her, his mouth devouring her very essence.

Brenna arched against the furs, pushing his face closer to her. Vali replaced his tongue with his fingers, his lips clamping over her sensitive nub. Her moans intensified as her body clenched around his fingers. As he took her over the edge, he felt as if she'd returned to him, body and soul.

Without giving her any time to recover, he knelt between her legs, pushing her thighs up. She was still hot and pulsing when he entered her, pushing himself in as far as he could. She grasped his wrists, still holding her thighs in place, as if to steady herself. He thrust in and out slowly, giving her a moment to adjust to his length. When she ground herself against him, he gave in to the desire that had grown wild with need; pumping her hard and fast. Her screams of pleasure washed over him until he felt the tightening deep inside his balls. Feeling Brenna contract around him, he let himself climb the wave and fall over its crest, calling her name as they both came undone together.

Hours later, Brenna's steady breath blowing softly across his chest, he tightened his arms around her. Sleep crept in to claim him while images of their future played out in his mind. Soon they would set sail for home, together.

---

13

*F*or the first time in many moons, Brenna's heart and head were light. Her body ached from the labour of battle, and as a reminder of the hours she'd spent with Vali. Her lips twitched into a smile, unbidden, at the memory of the pleasure they'd given each other.

Her return to Fornsigtuna had been delayed by a day, courtesy of Sigurd's second attack. However, her uncertain future didn't fill her with trepidation any more. Knowing Vali would provide her with a welcome distraction while she waited for the gods to reveal her fate was enough for now. Mayhap, Vali was her fate after all.

Walking through the marketplace on her way to the great hall, the whole town seemed to reflect her good mood. The battle had not reached the village and had merely halted the repairs from the first battle for a day. People went about their business, light hearted after vanquishing the would-be usurper once more. The forge, however, bore the brunt of the fight with warriors and farmers keen to replace or repair their weapons and tools.

Brenna would see to her weapons later that morning. Gita had cleaned them, but she alone would take responsibility for preparing them for the next battle. The servant girl walked behind her, waiting patiently each time Brenna was stopped along the way to recall a moment in yesterday's victory, or let her know a sacrifice to the gods would be made in her name.

The kindness and gratitude of Birca touched Brenna. Mayhap she had not been fated by the gods to rule here, but she had fought for this town and protected its people. Birca remained free and within the kingdom of Aric. That would be enough.

At last, they reached the great hall and went through to the private quarters. Brenna wanted to remove the last of her belongings and ensure Tarben's possessions were distributed to those warriors most deserving. The task would not take long and Brenna was pleased to find the bedchamber empty. She and Gita set about their work, Brenna issuing instructions to the servant when necessary and sending her to deliver Tarben's personal effects to his closest friends and advisors.

The sense of loss and fear that she felt the last time she'd made use of these chambers were gone. The disappointment of her marriage had been erased by battle, and then by Vali. She was no longer someone's burden to bear. And she hoped, no longer a prize to be bartered for favour or reward. Brenna inhaled, letting the breath cleanse her soul.

In this moment, she felt free.

"Fru?" Gita appeared in the doorway. "The King wants to see you."

She gave the girl a cheerful smile. She had not spoken with Aric since returning from battle and she imagined he wanted to hear firsthand how the battle to the east had played out.

"Thank you, Gita. Could you take the rest of these things to the longhouse?"

"Ja," she gave a brief nod as Brenna walked by.

The great hall had been full of slaves cleaning up after the previous evening's feast when she'd entered earlier. Now, she found the hall empty save for King Aric, sitting on the carved wooden chair that had been Tarben's. He was flanked either side by her father and Ubbe.

"Brenna," Aric held his arms wide but did not stand. "You are well, thank the gods."

"My King, Father," she nodded at each man. "Ubbe."

Ubbe's smile reached his eyes as he returned her greeting.

"Your instincts were correct," said Aric. "Sigurd had planned to sneak in and burn the town to the ground."

"Thank the gods he did not get that chance," said Brenna.

"Indeed," replied Aric.

"You were wise to send Ubbe and Brenna to the east, Sire," said Ragnar.

Brenna suppressed the smile that threatened to undermine her father's words, which were intended to soothe the King's ego at having her own theory proven true.

Everyone in this hall, in this town, knew it was she who had pre-empted Sigurd's battle plan.

"What of you plans now, King Aric?" asked Brenna. "Will you sail on the morro's tide?"

"Nei, we will delay for a few more days."

Surprise stirred Brenna's curiosity. She thought the King would want to return to Fornsigtuna as soon as possible, in the event Sigurd turned his attention there.

"I have decided that Ubbe shall be the new Jarl of Birca," declared King Aric.

Brenna turned to Ubbe. "A wise choice."

Her smile was genuine. Ubbe was a great warrior and would be a fair ruler. The townspeople respected and loved him as Tarben's nephew already. "May the gods guide you well, Ubbe."

Ubbe stepped closer, placing his hands on either side of her arms. "Thank you, Brenna." His voice was gentle, his eyes seemingly searching her face for something. "I know you hoped to rule alongside Jarl Beinersson," he said.

Uncertainty dulled her smile. She opened her mouth to protest, but Ubbe continued before she could speak. "And you have proven your loyalty to Birca and its people tenfold since his death. The people love you, Brenna. They call you Valkyrie because you protected them. They see who you are."

He paused a moment. "As do I."

Indignation boiled inside her. Did he think she needed it to be made clear to her that she would not be jarl? She took a breath and tried to steady her annoyance. She was returning to Fornsigtuna and his opinion mattered naught.

"I would respect you as my equal," said Ubbe. "You would rule by my side."

The argument she'd carefully constructed fled her mind. Ubbe still held her lightly, his smile was tender and hopeful. Confusion prevented her from understanding what he was saying.

"Brenna." She swung her gaze around to King Aric. "Ubbe has asked for your hand in marriage."

She looked to her father, who nodded his agreement. Ubbe traced his hands down her arms, taking her hand in his. Bewildered, she turned back to the new Jarl as he raised her hand to his lips.

"The wedding will take place in three days," announced the King with a clap of his hands.

14

---

*W*hat was happening? A moment ago, Brenna was set to return to Fornsigtuna with her lover. Now she was to stay on in Birca - and be married in three days!

All around, voices were talking at her. Competing with the silent scream in her head. Ubbe still held her hand. Servants appeared with horns of beer to toast the new Jarl of Birca. Warriors and members of council joined the cacophony. Brenna would rather face Sigurd and his army than suffer this moment. Her eyes jumped from face to face. Was Vali here? Did he know about this too?

Ragnar gave her a hard stare, raising his horn and encouraging her to drink and be merry. How had the horn gotten into her hand? She brought it to her lips, stopping short when the bitter smell assaulted her nose, turning her stomach. Ubbe had dropped her hand to accept the congratulations of his peers. Mayhap they spoke to her too. She could not comprehend what was happening.

When had this been planned? Last night while she'd be

feasting and drinking with the men and women she'd fought side by side with? None of those warriors need concern themselves with their future being sold off to another man while they celebrate their finest victory. Maybe it was during the hours after the moon had risen to its highest point, while she'd lain with Vali? Her heart stuttered in her chest. Who knew she'd been with Vali? It would not be a secret from those who wished to track her movements.

"Brenna?" Ubbe shook her slightly, staring into her eyes as if to drag her into the moment with him.

She opened her mouth but no words would form.

"Brenna," Ubbe spoke in hushed tones. "I would speak with you, in private?"

She nodded, anything to get out of this hall where the walls were closing in around her.

He led her back to the jarl's private quarters. With a start, Brenna realised the bedchamber she had just cleared of her belongings might once again hold her prisoner.

"You seem shocked by all that has transpired," began Ubbe.

"Of course, I'm shocked." Finally, her voice had resurfaced, along with her indignation. "I thought I was returning to my home and instead, I am once again bartered without consultation."

"You do not wish to rule Birca?" It was Ubbe's turn to be surprised.

"I do not wish to be married off without consideration for my own desires."

He seemed to consider this, his hand rubbing his jaw.

"I realise your marriage to Jarl Beinersson was... not ideal."

She grunted. Ideal was not a word she would ever use to describe her marriage.

"And that is not what I am offering."

"Offering?" Brenna spread her arms wide, her temper barely contained. "I heard no offer, Ubbe. I heard the King declare my fate as your wife."

"Is it not a fate you would consider worthy?"

She went to speak but he cut her off. "Brenna, you have proven to all that your mind is as sharp as your axe in battle, and your heart is true to Birca. I would not keep the Valkyrie of Birca caged and out of sight of the people. I meant what I said. I want you to rule at my side."

She swallowed the lump that had formed. "Those are but pretty words."

"Ja, they are but words."

He stepped towards her, reaching for her hand. She stepped back. Not yet prepared to concede. "Let me show you they will be more than words. It is my solemn oath to you."

He held her gaze with an intensity that sent a shiver up her spine. He was offering her the chance to rule and protect. She understood the people of Birca accepted her, but Ubbe was well-loved, he did not need her to consolidate his position as Jarl. He could have his pick of wives. Why her?

"And what of love?" she whispered.

A smile played across his lips, yet his eyes remained dark and unreadable.

"Love?" He cupped his hand to her cheek. His touch was hesitant, as if seeking permission for the intimate gesture. "I have long admired you, Brenna. I thought Tarben a fool to treat you as he did."

Ubbe traced his thumb gently across her cheek. "I would honour you and hope that in time, you might grow to love me too."

She brought her hand to cover his. Ubbe's were not as rough and calloused as Vali's sea-weathered hands. Nor was he as tall as Vali. But his smile was kind and his shoulders broad. Her heart hammered against her chest; her mind a jumble of incoherent thoughts. Could there be any truth to what Ubbe was proposing? What of Vali? This morning her heart had been full after being with him.

"I want to show you what our future would look like."

She frowned, uncertain where this was leading.

"I am meeting with the council to discuss the town's defences. I want you to join us."

Brenna stepped back, withdrawing from the flicker of wonder his touch had evoked. "Join you?"

"Ja. I would value your consideration of the various proposals."

She studied his face. "As Jarl, you would have the right to determine how the town is to be defended?"

"I would. But I would be a fool to think I could make the best decisions without hearing from others."

She waited for him to continue.

"You have an understanding of the people - their capabilities and their needs. Mayhap a better understanding than many of our greatest warriors." He began to pace. "You also have a good mind for battle and strategy. You are the one who predicted Sigurd would strike on two fronts."

"It is what I would do," she agreed. "And Sigurd's longboats had sailed in the opposite direction from which his land army approached."

"Exactly!" Ubbe's eyes shone with excitement. "You have a unique sense of strategy. One learnt at the heel of your father, mayhap?"

"I learnt to fight alongside King Aric's huscarl," she agreed.

"Ja, it is in your blood."

Her lips twitched as she acknowledged his praise and insight into her abilities. Mayhap she would not need to prove her worth to this Jarl. Yet, she could not shake the heaviness upon her shoulders. Once again, her fate had been determined without consideration or consultation. And her heart ached at the thought of losing Vali once more. Was this what the gods wanted from her? To set her heart aside in order to rule?

She glanced at Ubbe. He was every inch the warrior and the jarl that Birca needed. He spoke of kindness and mayhap, love? She drew in a shaky breath, wishing she could see her fate as the gods intended it.

"Will you come?"

She looked at Ubbe, unsure of his meaning.

"To meet with the nobles?" he clarified.

"Ja," she smiled at him, "I will come. But as a shield-maiden, not as your intended wife."

He tilted his head in silent question.

"If it is defensive strategies you wish to discuss, then I will come as a warrior."

Ubbe regarded her, his thoughts unreadable. Finally, he nodded. "As you wish, Valkyrie."

She gave a small sigh of relief as she turned to leave the room.

"If," said Ubbe, halting her steps, "by the end of the day, you still do not believe I want you as my wife and equal, I will go to Aric and withdraw my proposal of marriage."

She spun around to face him. "You would do that?"

"I want all of you, Brenna. I cannot live with anything less."

Understanding landed like a blow to her belly. He did not want a wife that loved another man. He did not want a wife who was not fully committed to him. For that, Brenna could not fault him. After all, that was all she had ever wished for herself.

15

"What makes you think Brenna will sail with us and not her father and the King?" asked Frode, each word underscored by the stroke of a whetstone against his axe. A light breeze blew across the fjord, taking the sting from the sun as Vali finished his appraisal of the longboat.

"Ah, Frode," said Vali, a cheeky grin on his face. "Brenna is the Valkyrie of Birca; the fiercest shieldmaiden in the land. She would rather sail with warriors."

Frode stopped sharpening his weapon to stare at his friend. "Aric and his huscarl are hardly cloth weavers."

"Nei, I mean Brenna is more like you and me, than the King and his entourage."

Frode chuckled, returning his attention to his axe. "Mayhap Brenna will think with her head and not her sex."

Vali landed his fist into Frode's arm, before stepping from the longboat onto the dock.

"So, you'll want a canvas erected for your sleeping quarters?" Frode called to Vali's retreating back, receiving a dismissive wave in answer.

Despite Frode's jibes, Vali couldn't shift the grin from his face. Brenna was coming home. Surely her success in the battlefield after these past months spent wasting away as the Jarl's wife had whet her appetite for more. Mayhap she was ready to sail the seas at his side?

Vali's good mood seemed to be mirrored in everyone he passed. People went about their business; selling, bartering, cleaning, cooking and working with a similar spring in their step. Birca had much to celebrate after their victories. And with the announcement of the new jarl expected from the King at any moment, another celebration would not be unwelcome.

"Vali?"

He surveyed the marketplace to discover where the voice had come from. Ragnar edged around some children re-enacting the battle with sticks between trading stalls. He kept his grin in place; not even Ragnar Eriksson could dampen his spirits.

"Well met, Vali."

"Well met, Ragnar." He gestured to the sky. "What a glorious day the gods have bestowed on us?"

"Ja," agreed the huscarl. "The gods continue to bless Birca."

They moved in the direction of the longhouses. Vali was a little uncertain as to why Ragnar had flagged him down. Mayhap word had gotten back to him about the night spent with his daughter? He was not concerned as his intentions for Brenna were honourable and he would let Ragnar know if that was his purpose. Regardless, Vali was not going to be the one to broach the subject.

"Has the King decided upon the new jarl?" he asked.

"Ja," said Ragnar. "Aric should announce it today." He

glanced around before leaning in closer to Vali. "It will be Ubbe."

Vali nodded. "Ubbe is a fine warrior and has the respect of the people. He is a good choice."

"I agree," Ragnar clapped him on the shoulder. "And the town will have twice the reason to celebrate."

"How so?"

"The wedding!" Ragnar brought his hands together. "The gods work in truly mysterious ways. Taking one jarl who did not honour his wife from Birca, then replacing him with another who will rule with the people's Valkyrie as his wife."

Vali halted in his tracks. "What?"

Ragnar faced him. "Ubbe and Brenna are to be married in three days."

The smile was wide across his face but his eyes betrayed the huscarl's true feelings. He knew exactly where Brenna had spent the night and he had come to make sure Vali knew he had no claim to his daughter.

His throat dried up and anger knotted his belly. Wishing he could knock the smug look off Ragnar's face with his fists, he gritted his teeth instead.

"We'll see about that." Vali stepped around the other man and made for his tent.

Ragnar may be Brenna's father but he did not know her heart. She would not be given away in marriage again, of that Vali was sure. He just needed to find her and they could set sail for Fornsigtuna on the evening tide. If she wasn't here, she couldn't be forced to marry the new Jarl. He would pack his belongings and let the crew know they were leaving tonight.

He shoved the canvas flap aside, kicking a discarded drinking horn as he entered. If Brenna had not found him by the time his furs were rolled and his weapons secured, he would go to the longhouse and find her himself.

"Vali Hrolfsson!" A deep voice spoke from outside the tent.

"Who wants to know?" he growled.

"King Aric requests you relieve the men patrolling the western border."

Vali stalked outside the tent.

"I don't answer to the King," he said to the huscarl standing in front of him.

"We all serve the King," came the swift reply. "Except for traitors."

Blood boiled in Vali's veins. He could not refuse an order from the King.

"There's a horse waiting for you at the stables. A huscarl will ride out with you." He turned on his heel and marched away, giving no opportunity for Vali to respond.

He grunted his frustration. There was no time to inform the crew, or find Brenna and let her know she did not have to bend to the wishes of her father and the King this time. It would have to wait until he returned from patrol.

BRENNA LEFT THE GREAT HALL, satisfied her opinions had been heard. Ubbe had kept his word and ensured her seat at the table was equal to that of everyone else. Nothing had been spoken of their intended marriage. As far as Brenna could tell, no one seemed to know of Ubbe's proposal.

A small sense of relief floated through her. If Ubbe was to withdraw from the marriage, no one in Birca would ever know. She could return to Fornsigtuna with Vali, and Ubbe could choose a new bride with his pride intact.

Still, nausea roiled her belly. This morning everything

had seemed so easy. She thought she'd known her fate. Now, she did not know which path to choose - or even if she would be given a choice. Ubbe had so far proven to be a man of his word. Would he let her go if that is what she really wanted? Would her father and King Aric allow him to let her go?

With her head down deep in thought, she paid no heed to anything around her. Strong arms gripped hers, stopping her in her tracks.

"Father? I did not see you."

"I could tell. Your mind was occupied elsewhere, Daughter."

The smile she managed was weak.

"What troubles you?" he dropped one arm, manoeuvring her towards the alehouse. "Although, I think I know."

They found a table easily; the day was still young and there was plenty of work to be done. Two tankards of mead were plonked on the table between them. Ragnar nodded his thanks at the servant before taking a large swig of the lukewarm liquid.

Brenna moved the tankard back and forth between her hands. She knew what was coming.

"The marriage to Ubbe is a good one. And is it not your right to claim your position as wife to the Jarl of Birca?"

He made it sound like being bartered was an honour.

"Is it not right that I should have some say in who claims me as their wife?" She gave her father a hard stare.

Ragnar chuckled. "And who would you choose, Daughter? The first man you bed after being widowed?"

Anger bristled up her spine. Of course, her father knew where she'd spent the night. His spies were everywhere.

"Who I bed is no concern of yours."

"Nei? Mayhap not last night or tonight. But once you're married to Ubbe you will stay loyal to your husband."

"I was always loyal to my husband. And I would be loyal again-"

"Good." Her father cut her off.

Brenna took a breath to try and steady her rising fury. "What if I do not want to marry Ubbe?"

Ragnar lowered his tankard and regarded his daughter for a moment. He shrugged.

Outrage burst along every vein and artery in her body. "I have done my duty to you and to Aric. Have I not earnt the right to choose for myself?"

"Daughter, you wanted to come to Birca. You wanted to be wife to the Jarl. This time, you would be more than a trophy. Ubbe is offering to have you rule by his side. What more could you want?"

She slumped down on the stool, her forehead leaning into her hand. He was right - in theory, it was what she'd wanted.

"What could Vali offer you that could sway you from your path?" Ragnar spoke in gentler tones.

"The freedom to choose," she said.

"Choose what? What would your life with Vali be?" He reached across and lifted her chin with the crook of his finger. "What is it you really want, Brenna?"

She opened her mouth but no words came out. The answer to that question was more difficult than she imagined. She wanted to be able to choose her own path, but which path was it that she wanted? She and Vali had not discussed what might happen upon their return to Fornsigtuna. They'd made no promises to each other. And sailing the seas in search of treasure still held no appeal to her. Would this mean she'd spend months alone, waiting for Vali to return to her? Hoping he would come home alive. What would she do while she waited?

Her head and heart continued their war. If Vali had never come to Birca, Ubbe would be offering her everything she believed she was destined for. But Vali had come to Birca.

There was also the question of could Ubbe's word be trusted. For the entirety of her marriage to Tarben, Ubbe had barely acknowledged her presence. He'd never shown any signs he admired her.

"Ah," said her father, breaking into her thoughts. "I see you do not know. Mayhap this decision is best left to those who are not so tormented by their emotions."

Squaring her shoulders, she looked her father in the eye. She had never been one to be ruled by her emotions over her intellect. Yet, she had no answer for his question.

"Ubbe has sworn to me he will withdraw his proposal if I do not desire the marriage."

"Be that as it may, the King has already made his decision."

She clenched her fists, nails digging into her palms, to keep her voice steady. "You would not speak for me, Father?"

Ragnar covered her closed fist with his larger hand. "If your heart and head aligned, and you truly did not want this marriage, I would speak for you."

Gratitude threatened to overwhelm her.

"But Brenna, if you cannot convince me that your path lies elsewhere, I will not agree for you against Aric."

"I understand, Father." Of course he would not risk the favour of the King for mere folly.

"You have until nightfall." Ragnar rose, planting a kiss on the top of her head and throwing some coins on the table before taking his leave.

She closed her eyes, seeking to still the conflict in her mind. "Allfather," she whispered. "I asked for this choice but now I know not what I should do. Please show me which of these paths has been fated as mine."

The chaos cleared and in her mind's eye she saw what she needed to do. Or rather, who she needed to speak with.

---

16

*V*ali rode his horse hard to meet the men he and the huscarl were to relieve from patrol. The terrain was still raw from the battle, hooves sinking into blood-soaked ground from which the bodies and debris had been removed. Vali passed the line of men and women returning from burying the defeated bodies, laden with discarded weapons and body armour. A translucent plume of smoke to the left of the battle field indicated where Birca had built the funeral pyres for their fallen warriors.

Occasionally a clump of green reached through the scarred and beaten land, more grass appearing as he rode passed the battleground. Muddy tracks showed where Sigurd's men had marched, thinking they were on their way to outsmarting Aric and his forces. They hadn't counted on Brenna seeing through Sigurd's plan.

The thought of Brenna spurred Vali on. He and the huscarl would meet the old patrol at the midpoint of Birca's border. From there they would head in opposite directions, on the lookout for any sign of intruders, before doubling back and repeating the process in the other direction. By the time they met in the middle again, the next patrol should have arrived and Vali could get back to the village and find Brenna.

The huscarls greeted each other and reported no sightings of Sigurd's army or his scouts. Vali gave his horse a chance to rest while the King's guards talked amongst themselves. The conversation held no interest for Vali as they spoke of fallen comrades and the return trip to Fornsigtuna.

Finally, the one they called Bjorn signalled to Vali that they should begin their patrol. Pulling himself up onto his mount, Vali nodded once before heading in the direction of Uppsala across the lowlands, leaving Bjorn to traverse the heavily forested hills and ridges. He nudged the horse into a canter, keeping his eyes peeled for movement in the distance.

Aric had stationed additional guards at the sacred site, so Vali expected his first patrol to be uneventful. With one eye on the countryside, he allowed his mind to turn over his encounter with Ragnar once more.

The older man had enjoyed ripping Vali's heart out with the news of Brenna's betrothal. He knew how Vali felt about Brenna, and that they'd been drawn together once more. Ragnar wanted more for his daughter and Vali knew why.

Hertha, Brenna's mother, was the cousin of Princess Ingrid; torn from her homeland and her people. Hertha, nor her father, had ever sought to have the throne returned to her bloodline, but that never stopped Brenna from dreaming of a future in which she might rule.

Aric and Ragnar had grown up together and a good marriage for his daughter was never in doubt. But Ragnar would not see Vali as worthy of his daughter, despite how hard he worked to provide for his family and his King. He was nothing more than a raider with no land or title. Sensing his growing frustration, the horse shuffled to the left, shaking its mane.

"Sorry, youngling," said Vali, stroking his neck. "It's not your fault."

It's Ragnar's, he thought. And Aric's. They'd taken her from him once before. Images of Brenna sitting stoically at the King's table, a mere ornament amongst men, warred with his memory of her laughing and drinking with her fellow warriors. Was her happiness worth nothing to them?

He could make her happy, he knew it. And given the choice, Vali was sure she would choose him this time.

When his horse drew alongside the border of Birca and Uppsala, Vali waited for the temple's guard to approach.

"What news of Sigurd?" called the guard.

"Nei," replied Vali, "there is naught. The temple?"

"The priests in the temple have been praying all day."

"Is that not their normal duty?"

"Ja, but this seems different." The guard shrugged. "Mayhap they are giving extra thanks for the King's victory."

Vali nodded. He hoped they were beseeching the gods for Aric to make better choices about the future Jarl of Birca and his intended bride. He turned his horse and headed back the way he'd come, keeping his eyes trained on the countryside.

Leaving the forested mountains of magnificent trees of maple, oak and ash, Vali manoeuvred his horse back through farming land. Before long he was once again amongst the broken fields of war. He passed the midpoint with no signs of the huscarl. Unease clenched in his gut. Looking into the distance, he saw no sign of an approaching horse, so the tension did not make sense. And yet, Vali trusted his instincts with absolute confidence. He urged his horse forward, hastening his pace.

Vali rode on through the lowlands, where there were little signs of life. The soil was of much poorer quality here and of no use to the farmers. Small clusters of pines and spruce broke up the landscape. A breeze rose as he drew closer to the sea, causing a gentle ripple through the branches.

A movement in the distance to his left stayed his roving gaze. It was almost naught, however its incongruence to the sway of the trees gave him pause. Tugging on the reign, he set the horse towards the copse, never shifting his eyes from the spot. The horse lifted his head and tail in unison, slowing his pace a fraction.

"You sense it too, youngling," murmured Vali, patting the animal's neck while tightening his grip on the reins with his other hand. "We're too exposed here. What do you say we call their bluff?"

With a final stroke of his mane, Vali pressed his heel into the horse. They set off at a gallop for the grove of pine trees, keeping his head low as a cover against whatever lay waiting for them.

As they came into the shadow of the trees, the horse reared up on his hind legs, spooked by the huscarl Bjorn, swinging his axe straight at them. Vali gripped the horn of the saddle, pulling his feet from the stirrups and slinging his legs to one side. He dropped to the ground, relying on the horse shielding him while he found his balance. What in the name of Thor was happening?

"Stop! I rode out with you to patrol," he yelled as his horse retreated and he was left exposed. Clearly this man thought he was someone else.

"I know who you are, Vali Hrolfsson," said Bjorn with

bloodlust in his eyes. "And you will not be returning from this patrol."

Vali leaned back to avoid the swing of Bjorn's axe. This man meant to kill him. On whose authority? Surely Ragnar would not stoop so low? He pulled his shield from his back and blocked the next attack just in time. The axe caught on the shield and Vali took the opportunity to kick his opponent in the chest.

Bjorn stumbled back, his axe dislodging itself and falling to the ground. Bjorn lunged for the weapon, but Vali was faster, stamping his foot upon the handle. He dropped the shield and unsheathed his dagger, holding it towards the throat of Bjorn.

"Who sent you to kill me?"

Bjorn snarled. He opened his mouth to speak as the thwack of an arrow hitting its mark sounded. Instead of words, blood trickled over Bjorn's lips.

"Sordinn!" Vali leapt to the side.

Movement in the trees behind the huscarl drew Vali's eye. Without hesitation, he threw the blade with all his might as the archer drew back a second arrow. The dagger struck the man's chest, pushing the arrow off target as he fell to his knees. Eyes bright with shock, the bow in the dead man's hand hit the ground a second ahead of his body.

Drawing his axe, he turned to find another man behind him. He swung the weapon at his head, glancing off the side. Vali stepped forward, easing the axe behind his head, readying to strike.

The other man threw down his own axe, hands raised in surrender.

"You must be one of Sigurd's," grunted Vali, unable to hide his disgust. "You throw down your arms the moment the fight gets too hard."

The man eyed his axe.

"It's too late for that," said Vali, moving in and placing his own axe against his dirty neck. "If I kill you now, you will die without honour."

He eyed the man he held at his mercy. "You're no warrior."

"Nei." The man tried to shake his head then thought better of it as the sharpened edge drew blood. "I ... I am a farmer."

"Sent by Sigurd the Black."

"Ja."

"Does Sigurd intend on returning to these shores?"

"Sigurd does not confide his intent in the likes of me."

Vali regarded the dirty rogue. He was black with mud and looked as though he'd not eaten a decent meal in days. The discarded axe was shorter than the ones usually wielded in battle. He probably spoke the truth, but it was not Vali's place to determine it one way or another.

He bound his captive's hands with rope and whistled for his horse to return. The horse had lost interest in the scene and had his head down, chewing on the foliage. Hearing Vali's whistle, he made his way over, stopping close to the two men and allowing Vali to secure his prisoner to the horn of the saddle with a length of rope.

Bjorn lay on his back, his unseeing eyes staring up at the occasional glimpse of sky through the ceiling of leaves. Vali quickly searched the man, looking for some clue as to who had sent the huscarl to kill him. He was Ragnar's man but he couldn't quite believe Ragnar would send another to do what he had threatened before Brenna's marriage to Jarl Beinersson. This was not Ragnar's style. But Aric, that was another matter entirely.

Vali mounted the horse and set off for Birca, forcing the

captured scout to jog to keep pace. Aric and his huscarls would soon find out how much the scout did or didn't know about Sigurd's plans.

And Vali would find Brenna and leave Birca before Aric found another opportunity to put an axe to his neck.

$\mathcal{B}$renna stood beneath the rocky incline, trying to gather a sense of whether her arrival would be welcome. The Seer lived on the outskirts of Birca, in a cave on the side of the mountain. The land surrounding his home was neither fertile for farming or welcoming for visitors. She supposed it served the ancient one's purpose, as Einar preferred to spend his time communing with the gods rather than guiding the paths of the living.

No one knew how old he was, only that he'd always been here. In his cave, outside Birca. His counsel was sought by many kings and warriors, but only given if they chose to climb the mountain. It was rare for Einar to be seen in the village, which made his appearance in the forest at Fornsigtuna and after Tarben's death all the more mystifying. Why had he sought her out? The gods had revealed something of her destiny to the Seer. Brenna needed to know which path she was fated to take.

The air was clean and fresh and she filled her lungs before starting her journey. Little by little she climbed up the stone, taking her time to find ledges for her hands and feet, cursing her skirt every time she stepped into it. Eventually the stone face gave way to smaller rocks jutting out of the earth. Pausing for breath, Brenna judged she was almost a third of the way into the climb. She examined her hands; her nails broken from battle and her palms rough from wielding her axe and sword. A thin line of blood ran through the dirt from a graze she opened up.They were the hands of a shieldmaiden. Were they the hands of a ruler?

Looking directly down into the village, all appeared well. She could see men and women working, children playing and longboats anchored in the fjord beyond. The rows of long buildings and the marketplace hid the wounds from the first battle. She wasn't yet high enough to see the scars inflicted on the landscape from the second fight.

Brenna felt a tug of pride as she considered her adopted home. There was room for the village to grow. For more traders to base themselves at the gateway to the Baltic trade route. Birca was already attracting more and more merchants looking to trade their treasures for the iron, skins, horns and furs the town was known for. Gazing around the outer reaches of the village, Brenna could picture the types of fortifications they would need to build to keep their enemies out. Mayhap she would suggest to Ubbe they ride out along the borders and discuss her ideas.

Her heart lurched. Was Ubbe a man of his word? She wanted to believe he was, not just for her sake, but for the people who lived in his jarldom. Her thoughts began to compete with her heart again. Raising her eyes to the fjord, images of Vali invaded her mind. He was a man of his word; of that she was certain. He'd been her friend and confidante since her childhood. Now he was her lover. Warmth spread through her; memories of their bodies joined in passion almost threatened to erase all other considerations.

Allowing a shudder to run through her and relieve her growing anxieties, Brenna shook her hands out and hitched her skirt before starting to climb again. The next stage of the journey was not as taxing, with bigger footholds and more rocks to hold on to. She kept her thoughts focused on the climb, while she moved closer to the cave.

Finally, the ascent evened out and she was able to walk the last of the way. Boulders enclosed all but a small opening in the mountainside. Empty baskets that once contained food and other offerings led her to the entrance. Brenna wondered who in the village made this climb regularly to bring the Seer nourishment. Mayhap the women-folk might take her into their confidence if she stayed and allow her to discover the town's secrets.

"I wondered when you'd come."

The voice was clear, but distant. Brenna couldn't be sure the sound hadn't come from inside her own head; as before when Einar had spoken to her from across the battlefield.

"I thought you would have sought me out much sooner after your husband's death," the voice continued. "To know the ways of the gods."

Brenna stepped into the darkness, letting her eyes adjust before moving forward towards the faint orange glow.

"It seems you were distracted by your bodily desires." A slow laugh, neither malicious nor jovial, echoed through the chamber.

She placed her hand on the cool, dry stone to guide her path.

"And the small task of defending the town from a second attack from Sigurd the Black," she replied to the shadows.

"Ja, the Valkyrie of Birca has been busy justifying her reputation on the battlefield."

"My reputation was the least of my concerns."

"Nei?"

The tunnel she'd been following opened up into a cavern. The Seer sat beside the fire pit, his face shrouded by the black linens he wore over his head and around his body. Behind him, skins and furs made up his sleeping area. Bones and feathers were placed all round; the remnants of offerings to the gods and protection from what Einar saw in his visions.

"You didn't hunger for acknowledgement from your husband? From his people?"

Brenna regarded the Seer, unsure what he meant.

"Your value has been determined by your abilities as a shieldmaiden. Your skills on the battlefield have given you the opportunity to show the people who you are, Brenna of Fornsigtuna. Valkyrie of Birca."

The measured timbre of his voice revealed what she knew in her heart to be true.

"Sit," he instructed. "You have many questions."

"I seek only one answer." She sat opposite him, folding her legs beneath her.

"Hmm," Einar grunted. His blackened mouth and teeth were contrasted by the sickly pallor of his skin. His eyes remained under the hood. Cadaverous fingers reached for a pouch next to the fire pit. Tipping the contents out, bones carved with the symbols of the gods fell on the dirt between them.

"You wish to know your fate, Valkyrie."

She nodded.

"Mayhap it is your destiny you should be more concerned with."

"Fate is what will lead me to my destiny."

"There is an order to the world. The gods have determined our fate."

"Ja, the gods know what is fated for each of us," she agreed.

Einar ran his hand over the bones, pausing every so often to push and poke at them, as if they had chosen to defy the message they were to deliver.

"It is our actions that shape our destiny, Valkyrie."

"I don't understand," she whispered.

"You believe your mother was destined to be a Queen, and yet her fate brought her to another path."

Her hands curled into fists. "She could have been Queen of Gyldarhagi, the last of her family."

The Seer raised his head from studying the bones. "And yet," spittle glistened his blackened lips, "she is not."

Her ingrained indignation shivered up her spine. Then it was gone. Replaced by an understanding that her mother's destiny was not hers to avenge. The gods had delivered her fate and it was not Brenna's right to question it.

"What of *your* destiny, Valkyrie?" Einar interrupted her thoughts.

"My destiny?"

"What is it you desire above all else?"

He had returned his gaze to the bones, his hands still running over them, divining their intention.

"I wish to rule."

His hands stilled.

"I wish to protect my people and ensure their prosperity through trade and farming rather than conquest."

The ancient one nodded.

"If that is the destiny you desire, Valkyrie, then you need

not trouble yourself with fate. You must trust the gods to know what lies ahead."

Although she did not doubt the truth of his words, it helped her naught with the choice she must make today. Nor did it help with making sense of what the Seer had told her all those years ago.

"And what of my ancestors?" Her words were barely a whisper.

Einar flicked his tongue across his lips. "As you said, it is your destiny to rule, to protect your people and right the wrongs of the past." He breathed heavily, a whine emanating from deep inside him.

An energy, a bolt of lightning, tore up her spine sending her equal measures of terror and pain.

"Your ancestors have waited long for you, Valkyrie. Fulfil your destiny, no matter the cost."

She opened her mouth to ask more and was silenced by the Seer's hand, offered to her palm up. There was nothing more he would say. To push for anything more would only offend the Seer, and the gods.

She took his hand in her palm, running her tongue from his fingertips to his wrist.

The sunlight blinded her as she left the cave, forcing her to wait until her senses returned before beginning her descent. The fresh air cleared her mind, leaving her own words running over and over. She wanted to rule. More than that, she wanted to rule Birca.

Brenna could not see a way in which refusing Ubbe would deliver her this destiny. Love was important. She wanted what Ragnar and Hertha had, what she had grown up with. But love alone, was not enough. Not for Brenna. Especially when she could not see her destiny coming to fruition if she chose Vali.

Vali wanted to conquer other lands, and mayhap he would come to rule those lands. That was not Brenna's way. She wanted to protect, not conquer. Trade, not plunder.

Her heart ached with the understanding that in order to fulfil the destiny she wanted, she would need to let Vali go. That was the cost she must bear. She could only pray that in time, her heart would know love again.

18

A sense of anticipation ran through the air as Vali joined the throng of people moving towards the great hall. He'd sent the first huscarls he met to replace him on patrol. Now he wished he'd asked for one of them to accompany him through the town. Vali coaxed the horse through, pulling the rope and his captive closer to his side. The last thing he needed was for the crowd to take their vengeance out on Sigurd's scout.

He spotted Gunnar moving towards him. Pointing the horse in the direction of the stables, Vali motioned for the huscarl to meet him there. Dismounting, he stretched his back from side to side, pleased to get out of the saddle. With his dagger, he cut the rope joining his prisoner to the horse. A stable hand ran out to take the horse to be fed and watered.

"Well met, Vali," said Gunnar. "What do we have here?"

"Well met, Gunnar." He shoved the man forward. "A gift for the King."

Gunnar eyed the man, who was in no hurry to stand after falling to the ground.

"I found him and another on the southern border. Scouts of Sigurd."

"What of the other?"

"Dead."

"And Bjorn?"

"Felled by the scout's arrow." It was the truth and Vali felt no need to mention the confrontation that occurred prior to his death. He would only bring more trouble upon his shoulders if he were to accuse the King of wanting him dead.

Gunnar grunted. Bending down he pulled the captive's head up by his hair, forcing him to look him in the eye.

"What do you know of Sigurd's plans?"

He moaned in response.

"He said he knows naught, he was only sent to spy and report back."

Gunnar dropped his grasp, the head hitting the dirt hard. The huscarl wiped his hands together.

"Spies know more than they are told. That's why they are spies." He grinned at Vali. "You should head over to the great hall. Our King is to announce the new jarl."

Two more huscarls appeared, wrenching the scout to his feet.

Vali swallowed the bile that rose in his mouth. He hoped that was all the King was announcing. With a nod to Gunnar, he joined the swell of people making their way to the hall, managing to slip inside as Aric rose to address the people.

"Brothers and sisters," he began. "We have fought off our enemy, not once, but twice. And we have been victorious."

"Thank the gods," rippled through the crowd.

Vali leaned against the wall. Ragnar was not at the King's

side. He scanned the room but could not place him. Mayhap he'd gone to question the scout himself.

"But it has not been without great sacrifice and loss," continued Aric. "The Allfather saw fit to call Jarl Beinersson to Valhalla. And while he feasts in the Golden Hall, we are left to fill his place."

The curtain separating the private quarters from the hall was pushed aside, revealing Ragnar and Brenna. Brenna seemed to be trying to speak with her father. Ragnar raised his hand, demanding silence and jerking his head towards the dais on which the King stood. Vali's gut tightened and his heart raced. He'd not returned in time.

"It is only fitting that one of you take up the mantle of jarl, for who else knows the people of Birca as well as one of your own." Aric gestured and Ubbe stepped up to join him.

"Ubbe is the nephew of Tarben Beinersson. He is of noble bearing. He is a great warrior."

The crowd was nodding and murmuring their agreement. Vali breathed in heavily. He couldn't deny Ubbe's credentials.

"I present to you, Ubbe, the new Jarl of Birca," proclaimed King Aric to the roar of approval from the people.

Horns of beer were produced and downed to the cheer of "Skal!" After a few moments, the King called for quiet.

"Tonight, we will make a sacrifice to the gods and then feast in honour of the new Jarl."

Stamping and cheering broke out again. Aric motioned that he was not finished.

From the corner of his eye, Vali saw Ragnar push Brenna forward toward the dais. She turned, as if to resist, but Ragnar stood firm. Vali straightened his stance, his senses on alert.

"We have much to celebrate." Aric turned to face Ubbe. Brenna was now at his side, with Ragnar standing close by.

"In two days, we will celebrate the wedding of Jarl Ubbe to the Valkyrie of Birca!"

Excitement bounced off the walls. The cheering was twice as loud. People rushed forward to congratulate Ubbe and Brenna, encircling them in a web of bodies. Before he lost sight of her, Vali was sure he saw a flash of anger in her eyes. He cursed under his breath.

Surely, they would not do this to her again. They would not force her to marry the Jarl, force her apart from him. Or did Aric believe the problem solved? Mayhap word had not yet reached him of Bjorn's demise.

Outrage coursed through his veins. He would not let this stand. He had to get to her. They could escape. Right now. They could go over land, head towards the Baltic region. The crew could meet them.

With his mind made up, Vali started to push his way through the crowd. He just needed to get Brenna's attention. To signal to her to come to him as soon as she could get away. They'd soon be busy preparing for the sacrifice. She would have a chance to slip away. He had to be ready.

A heavy hand gripped his shoulder. Turning, he found Gunnar holding him steady.

"The King has asked to see you," he shouted above the din.

Vali glanced back to the dais. Aric was nowhere to be seen.

"He wants a first-hand account of the scouts you came upon."

He was sure Aric wanted a first-hand account of Bjorn's death and anything the huscarl may have said to Vali. Surely bringing the scout in would halt any murderous plans the King had for him? For a little while, at least. He looked to the dais one more time. Brenna and Ubbe were still surrounded by people. He had no hope of catching her eye.

"Vali! The King is waiting."

"Ja," he said, resigning himself to following Gunnar. "I'm coming."

BRENNA STOOD ON HER TOES, straining to see if Vali was somewhere in the great hall. Nothing had gone to plan. Neither Ubbe nor her father had waited for her answer. Now there was no way she'd have a chance to speak with Vali before he heard that she was promised in marriage to Ubbe. Anger coursed through her, draining the colour from her face and reason from her tongue. She needed to keep silent until she had the opportunity to talk to Ubbe alone.

Two figures moving toward the main doors snagged her attention. Vali! He must have heard the King announce the engagement. And now he was leaving without speaking to her. Would he ever speak to her again?

A tankard full of mead was thrust into her hands. Blindly, she smiled her thanks and took a long draught. She was grateful Ubbe was receiving most of the attention. Men gave him hearty slaps of congratulations on his elevation to Jarl, and his impending marriage. Her knuckles whitened as she clutched the tankard. She must speak with Ubbe.

The King and her father had disappeared. Mayhap they were issuing instructions in preparation for the sacrifice in Ubbe's honour? Aric was hardly the kind of man to step aside and let another have all the adoration. If he and her father could absent themselves, so could she and Ubbe.

Reaching for his forearm, she plastered a smile on her face. "Ubbe, we need to prepare for the ritual."

She swallowed hard and prayed she looked unconcerned by all that had taken place. She had no desire to make Ubbe look the fool in front of his people. There was every chance Ubbe had not known of the King's plan to announce their marriage. She must give him an opportunity to explain what he knew of this before she judged him harshly.

He covered her hand with his. "Of course." His smile reached his eyes. "There is much to do."

With nods of thanks and acknowledgement to their well-wishers, he led Brenna back to the private chamber behind the curtain. Once inside, she pulled her hand free and walked ahead, needing a moment to breathe and compose her thoughts.

"That went well," said Ubbe.

"Ja, the people are well pleased you are to be their Jarl."

"They are pleased there will be a wedding and all the feasting that goes with it," he chuckled.

"Ubbe," she turned to face him. She needed to look into his eyes and know the truth. "I had not given you my answer. Nor had I indicated to my father what my answer would be."

Ubbe stepped forward, taking her hands in his. "It matters naught."

She tilted her head to the side. "What do you mean?"

"The decision had been made. We are to be married."

The smile on his face appeared to morph into a sneer. His hands suddenly felt clammy on her skin.

"You gave me your word, Ubbe." Her heart beat thundered between her ears. "You said if I did not wish for this marriage you would go to the King and withdraw your offer."

"Brenna," the smile leached from his eyes. "Do you really believe the King and your father would care if you did not wish for this marriage?"

"I thought you would care," she whispered.

He withdrew his hands and walked to the bench to pour himself some mead.

Brenna stood, her hopes turning inside out.

"I understand," Ubbe's tone was low and even. "That your decisions are being guided by your cunny at present. A situation I have sought to have remedied."

Brenna gasped. "How dare you?"

"How dare I?" He looked at her with pure hatred. "I believe you will come to see the wisdom in our match. Not just for Birca, but for your own ambition."

Slamming the tankard on the bench, he crossed the room in two strides. Grabbing her chin between his thumb and forefinger, he squeezed hard enough for tears to threaten.

"Unlike your first husband, you will find I want you in my bed. And I will take my fill of you every night."

He let her go. She refused to step back, to show weakness. She kept her chin high while she forced back the tears. They glared at each other for a moment until Ubbe drew in a deep breath.

"I apologise, Brenna. It is not my intention to hurt you. I am angry."

She held her stare, her own anger simmering dangerously close to the surface.

"The thought of another man touching you... I cannot bear it." She opened her mouth but could not get a word out. "I know, you were not sworn to me and you had endured Tarben for many moons. I do not blame you." He stepped close again. "But no more, Brenna. You are to be my wife and you will never see him again. I have made sure of that."

She closed her mouth. She needed time to think. Time to put the pieces of the last hour together in her mind and understand what that meant for her. And to let Vali know he was in danger.

*V*ali finished recounting his skirmish with Sigurd's scouts to the King. Aric insisted Vali repeat the story to Ragnar, who was with the prisoner. They appeared to accept that Bjorn and Vali had been ambushed by the scouts, resulting in Bjorn's death. That Aric did not question why they were together so far from the midpoint of the patrol only fuelled Vali's suspicions. Blood boiled in his veins.

Finally, there was nothing more to say, no other way to consider the events. The time had drawn nigh for the ritual to ask the blessing of the gods for Ubbe's appointment as Jarl. Aric would officiate and Ragnar would be his ever-present self. Brenna would be there - what other choice would she have? Questions would be asked if Vali failed to show his face.

As Vali returned to his tent, the town was buzzing with excitement. Despite the losses and pain of battle, the people found plenty to celebrate. Tonight was an important celebration, but it would not rival the upcoming wedding.

He washed and changed his clothes. By the time he 'd

made his way back to the clearing in front of the great hall, the ritual had begun.

The crowd quietened as King Aric stepped forward into the middle of the gathered townspeople. He wore a white under-tunic, covered by a plain brown robe and his only adornment was his ceremonial helmet. A huscarl stood closely with a cow tethered by a rope around its neck. Aric raised his arms and began to speak.

"Tonight, we honour the gods and ask their continued blessing on Birca and all who reside here. We ask the gods to bless Jarl Ubbe of Birca. Hail Allfather, Hail Grimnir, Hail Gangleri."

His words echoed over the silent crowd.

"Lord of the Einherjar. God of Wisdom and Poetry and Battle. Son of Borr and of Bestla."

A shiver of anticipation rippled through the air.

"You who reside in Valhalla. You who is the wisest of the nine realms and gave to us the Runes. Wielding the mighty Gungnir in our defence."

Aric took the axe offered to him and stepped up to face the cow. Raising the axe above his head, he continued.

"I honour you."

Vali watched as the axe struck the cow between the eyes, blood splattering over the King and those standing closest.

"Hail Odin."

"Hail Odin," the crowd repeated.

Replacing his axe with a knife, Aric slit the cow's throat. As the animal's legs buckled, a bowl was placed beneath the cut, catching the blood as it spilled.

The cow fell to the ground and the bowl was pulled free. The King took a switch and dipped it into the blood. Ubbe stepped forward as he approached - blood spattered across his face and clothes. The King continued to shake the switch so that all present had a chance to receive the sacred blood.

Already, the cow was being butchered into smaller pieces that would be roasted over fire pits and served up later in the evening. Servants appeared with full horns of beer and tankards of mead. Aric raised his horn in toast.

"To the Allfather."

His words were repeated and the vessels drained. Servants quickly refilled each one. Ubbe held his horn aloft next.

"To the King and his continued victories against his enemies."

"To the King!"

Noblemen stepped forward to offer their own pledges for future victories. Farmers pledged their honour to the gods in exchange for prosperous harvests. Merchants and raiders swore their own oaths. Vali retreated to the safety of his crew. His fealty remained intact, but his pride prevented him from giving his pledge. He'd given Aric and Ubbe enough today.

As the sun set, beer and mead continued to flow while hunger was kept at bay with cheese and bread until the meat was roasted. Vali sipped at his beer, the bitter liquid churning with the rising acid in his gut. Around him, men talked and laughed, drank and ate. He nodded occasionally and chewed slowly on a cut of roasted beef. Suspicions rolled around his head, his temper barely contained.

Ubbe was the centre of attention and he appeared to relish the adulation of the townspeople as they jostled for favour and position with the new Jarl. Aric and Ragnar were right in the mix, encouraging the congenial rivalry.

"You look set to take up weapons and challenge the Jarl

for his position." Frode stood close, so only Vali could hear him. "Mayhap it's his bride you would prefer to win?"

Vali's anger surfaced as a growl. Throwing the last of his meat into the fire and downing the dregs of his beer, he rose to his feet. Frode stood and put his hand on Vali's shoulder.

"T'was a jest, Vali," he said. "Not a suggestion."

"You think me so foolish as to challenge Ubbe on the night he is proclaimed Jarl?"

"Nei," said Frode. "I think you angry enough to forget yourself."

Beneath the warning in Frode's eyes was a flash of fear. The crew would have his back, even if Vali was stupid enough to raise a sword to the Jarl. But they all knew they would pay for their loyalty with their lives. Despite the rage and frustration coursing through his body, Vali would never put his men in that situation.

"I've seen enough and I am tired," said Vali, keeping the anger from his voice. "I'm to bed."

Frode held his stare for a moment before giving him a nod and moving out of his path.

VALI LEFT THE FEAST, walking on the edge of the darkness so as not to be drawn into the tall tales and laughter of the townsfolk. He'd not seen Brenna in some time. He'd stayed toward the back of the hall with his crew, hoping she might slip away from the revelry and find a moment to speak with him. When Brenna stayed away, it only fuelled his anger and suspicious mind more so.

By the time he arrived at his tent, he had convinced himself Brenna must have agreed to the engagement. Why else would she be avoiding him? He cast the flap aside with enough force to cause the figure waiting inside to jump.

"Brenna!" The sight of her dispelled all his previous emotion.

"I thought you'd never return." She stepped toward him, and the rose oil scent of her hair was immediately soothing.

"I looked for you but Frode said you were out on patrol?" She laid her hands on his chest.

"Ja, there was some trouble on the borders. Sigurd's scouts." His arms encircled her waist. "I got back in time to hear of your engagement."

"Vali, I did not agree to this engagement." Her eyes begged him to believe her. His body sagged in relief. "I did not know the King was going to announce-"

He covered her mouth with his own. Vali only cared that Brenna was with him, in his arms. He tasted the mead on her soft, full lips. Probing deeper with his tongue, he tasted her innate sweetness. She responded in kind, her tongue exploring his mouth, a moan catching in her throat. Her arms slipped around his neck, her hands grasping his hair. He pulled her tighter, needing to be closer still.

The fire in his belly turned his blood molten, his loins tightening as desire raged through him. He pulled at her fastenings as her fingers slipped beneath his tunic, freeing it from his trousers. They broke apart to remove their clothing. Breanna laid back against the furs, half-light bathing her naked body. He took a moment to admire her curves, her muscled frame under soft skin.

Her eyes skimmed over his body, coming to rest on his cock, erect in his hand. Kneeling, Brenna reached for him and he relinquished his grip so she could touch him as she wished. The palm of her hand was gentle as she ran it along his length. He closed his eyes and focused on the sensation of her fingers tightening around his width, her other hand cupped his balls. With slow, languid strokes, she took control.

The heat from her mouth preceded her tongue for a second. She circled the tip of his cock, her hand continuing to hold him in place. Threading his hands through her hair, he opened his eyes to find her looking up at him through her lashes.

"By the gods," he groaned, her eyes never leaving his as her mouth descended down his shaft. Her hands wrapped around his buttocks as she took more of him into her mouth, rocking her head back and forth, her tongue moving over and under.

He rode the wave closer and closer to its crest, his breathing ragged with want.

"Not yet," he growled, pulling her hair back until his cock sprang free. Plundering her mouth with his tongue, he tasted the traces of his own essence.

Carnal passion overrode all his senses. Pushing her roughly back against the furs, he spread her legs wide before him, running his hand up her thigh until he reached her glistening mound. He traced a finger over her slit, finding her warm and wet.

Brenna gasped as his fingers stroked her. She bit her lip then pushed his hand against her, grinding against him.

"Vali," she whispered, her eyes full of need.

Holding her gaze, he ran his tongue around his mouth, letting her imagine what he planned for her next.

"Please," she breathed.

He gripped her buttocks and lavished his mouth on her, devastating her with his tongue. She cried out to the gods, begging for release. As he felt her quiver against his tongue, he pulled back. Flipping her onto her stomach, he held her hips and dragged her onto her knees. She raised herself up against him, twisting around to press her lips to his own.

Her skin was silky smooth as he ran his hands up and over her. Cupping a breast in each hand he massaged them before taking both nipples between his fingers, pulling and plucking at them. Brenna ground her arse into his groin and he responded in kind.

Pushing her onto all fours, he positioned himself at her entrance, her heat sending currents of primal lust through him. He pushed himself part way in, her sex wet and wanting. Reaching up, he grasped her hair, pulling it tight as he rammed his cock in hard.

Brenna whimpered while he held her in place. He withdrew, then ploughed inside her again.

"More," she panted.

Needing no more encouragement, Vali drove himself in and out of her, harder and faster. His belly tightened and he growled as he felt himself rise on the wave again. Her moans were guttural, her own need as desperate as his. He felt her clench hard around his cock as he sent them both over the edge.

———————

aces swarmed around her. Tarben, Ubbe, Aric, her father... the Seer. She looked for Vali but he wasn't there. She tried to speak with those around her, to reason with them. They would pull back, refusing to hear her. Their voices echoed over the top of each other, hurting her ears with their booming assault. No one was talking to her, only about her. Fear and frustration warred within her. The sights and sounds were suffocating. She couldn't get air into her lungs.

"What of your destiny, Valkyrie?" Einar's words sounded inside her head.

She turned, trying to find the voice. The Seer was far away, only his voice was close. Too close.

"I want..." she tried to speak but she had no breath.

"It doesn't matter what she wants."

Who said that?

"Her fate has been determined by the gods," said Einar.

"She is my daughter to command."

Father?

"You command her. Her husband commands her. But her path is fated."

Her head ached. She needed oxygen.

"What of your destiny, Valkyrie?"

"My dest..." she tried to force the words. "I want..."

The Seer banged his staff into the earth. The noise was deafening, banishing everything else.

"Your destiny?"

She straightened. Her thoughts started to fall into order.

"Brenna!" Another voice broke through. Her body shook.

"Brenna, wake up!"

Her eyelids fluttered, still heavy with tormented visions. As consciousness returned, a weight sat on her chest. Her eyes flew open and she sprang forward. She inhaled and oxygen raced into her lungs in time with her racing heart. Dirty, white canvas pressed in around her and she waited for the faces to appear.

"Brenna?" The voice was softer now. Hands rubbed her shoulders.

Her breathing echoed in her head.

"Brenna?"

She turned to the voice. *Vali.*

The adrenaline leached from her, leaving her nauseous and shaking. She leaned her head against his shoulder.

"You're okay," he whispered against her hair. "It was just a dream."

She nodded, letting him take her into his arms. It was true that she'd defied Ubbe in coming here, and she cared naught. Ubbe had shown a darker side of himself that had cast a pall over everything she thought she wanted. Was this the fate the gods had in store for her, to be with a man who did not honour his word?

The man whose bed she was sharing brought her

comfort. It was a comfort she needed tonight. But what of tomorrow, and the day after? Her thoughts bounced from one scenario to another.

She could not stomach the thought of another loveless marriage. Would Ubbe renege on everything he'd promised her? It was possible he needed her and her strategic mind. She'd never known him to have strong beliefs regarding the future of Birca. He'd always done as he was bid by Tarben. Mayhap he'd played his cards close to his chest in order to protect his interests. Should Ubbe's actions dissuade her from her destiny?

Brenna let Vali pull her down into the warmth of his furs. He stroked her forehead, soothing her troubled thoughts and lulling her into a dreamless sleep.

BRENNA WOKE as the sun began its ascent over the mountains. Beside her, Vali slept soundly, his chest rising and falling in an even tempo. In his sleep, he reminded her of the boy she'd grown up with. When they had the whole world at their feet and a lifetime of adventure ahead of them. Before politics and position became her guiding force.

It would be so easy to wake him with kisses feathered along his jaw, a gentle nip at his earlobe. To dress and make their way to the docks, sneak away and start a different life. Brenna imagined it could be quite idyllic - for a time. Before reality set in, Vali left her to raid on foreign shores. He might convince her to join him.

No, raiding would only remind her of her distaste for it. Which means she would have to wait; but where would they live? In Fornsigtuna? Her father and the King would never allow it. They'd be forced into exile. Ubbe may not give her up so easily. Mayhap he would hunt them down and take back what had been promised to him.

She sighed internally, raising her eyes to the gods above. If only they'd given her a clear sign of what she should do. Mayhap, they just did.

To run away with Vali would only bring heartache. For both of them. For his family. Her mother. Her destiny seemed to grow farther away the longer she lingered in his furs.

Rising, she found her clothes and dressed. With her hair loose and hiding her face, she hurried back to the long-house she'd shared since the death of Tarben. Her decision weighed heavily on her heart. Even as she knew it was right.

21

*L*ight surrounded him, and flowed through him. In the moment between sleep and wakefulness, Vali felt at peace. Stretching into the space beside him, he opened his eyes to find he was alone. Again.

There was no trace of her. Had she left of her own accord? Hastily, he threw his trousers and tunic on. Taking a moment to lace his boots and sheath his dagger at his side. At any other time, he'd have bathed in the fjord, or at least washed the sleep from his face, but he needed to find Brenna and ensure her safety. It was inconceivable she'd leave without speaking with him.

He walked through the makeshift tents towards the longhouses. He'd slept later than was his habit. The whole village was already about their day as he weaved through children playing and women hauling washing towards the river. In the distance, he could hear the sounds of the marketplace - traders selling their wares and locals haggling for better prices. The crash and clang of iron at the forge added to the undercurrent of the village at work.

He approached the longhouse Brenna had moved into.

A woman swept the floor while others tended to the sleeping quarters, shaking out the skins and furs. Vali stood awkwardly in the doorway, not sure if he expected to find Brenna helping with the domestic chores. From the opposite end of the room, a familiar figure appeared.

"Gita," he stepped forward only to have his progress halted by the servant's gesture to wait outside.

Vali complied, backing out into the daylight.

"You shouldn't be here," hissed Gita when she joined him.

"I'm looking for Brenna, I must speak with her."

"Nei!" The servant girl crossed her arms, her eyes fierce.

"Gita," her tone made him wary, "is she well?"

"She does not want to speak with you."

Vali's hackles rose. "I do not believe that is true."

He went to move around the servant and see for himself. Gita stepped across his path. "Nei, Vali."

"Gita, where is she?"

Her eyes betrayed her, glancing towards the great hall.

"Ubbe? He took her?" Panic and anger rose inside.

"Nei," the girl reached for his arm. "She went to Ubbe."

She must have had no choice. "I will bring her back."

Gita sighed, tightening her grip. "Vali, she went to Ubbe to tell him she would marry him."

The noise and sights around him faded to nothing. "Nei, she would not," he whispered.

She nodded. "Ja, Vali. It is true."

She waited a beat, as if to see if her words would sink in. "Vali, you cannot follow her. The Jarl will have you sent away, or worse."

"Worse?" he narrowed his gaze.

"Ubbe knows that Brenna went to you," she stepped closer and muttered into his ear. "It is you who is not safe."

Indignation turned his vision red. "He would not dare threaten me."

"He would do more than that," mumbled Gita.

Vali pulled his arm free. Could Ubbe be the one who sent Bjorn? Now Ubbe must have made threats against him and Brenna agreed to the wedding only to save him from the axe.

"I'll not have Brenna marry him to save my head."

"That's not why she's doing it," Gita called as he turned away. "She is the Valkyrie of Birca. She means to rule by his side."

It hit him harder than any axe. Brenna had always wanted to rule; it was in her blood. More than any love she felt for him.

HE TURNED ON HIS HEEL, walking blindly through the long-houses until he reached the fields. On some level he knew he was retracing his steps from the battle, when he'd followed Brenna to war. Believing in her. Wanting to be near her. The shock he'd felt just moments ago was being dissolved by his fury. He veered to the left, taking him away from the path that led to the battle grounds, towards the rocky mountain.

As the mountain loomed before him, Vali decided to press on. He needed to keep moving, to push himself. He didn't trust himself with a sword to spar with his men. And Odin help him if he came across Aric or Ragnar. Twice now, both men had stood in the way of what he knew in his heart to be his fate. Nei, he needed to work his aggression out in a way that wouldn't end with an axe at his throat.

He began the climb, forcing himself to move fast, not looking for shortcuts. Focus on not falling, that was what he wanted. The physical exertion was pushing Brenna from his consciousness. Get to the top. Then he could think things through.

The sun was at its height in the sky, blinding him to all but the terrain directly in front of him. Sweat trickled down his back and face, stinging his eyes. More than once, his foot slipped, sending his heart racing and his fingers scrabbling to hang on while he found more stable ledges of rock. By the time the ground evened out, he was wet from perspiration and bloody and dirty from the climb.

Reaching a landing, he sat against a rock, hands on his knees, and filled his lungs with air. Beneath, Birca lay spread. It was a beautiful sight. The town had expanded in recent years thanks to increased trade from the East. Farmers continued to work the small parcels of land upon which crops could grow. Further ahead, the fjord sparkled like a sea of diamonds. Men on the docks scurried like ants.

"A land worthy of a Valkyrie's rule."

The voice came from nowhere, rumbling slowly. Vali jerked around. A tall, thin creature shrouded in black stood along the path, his staff in hand. Einar; the Seer of Birca.

"I could feel your anger from my cave, Styrimaðr," said the Seer.

Vali shifted his gaze back to the distant fjord, his surprise at the Seer's sudden appearance abating. "'Tis not unbelievable. I have plenty of anger."

A slow chuckle reverberated off the mountain. "Your anger is misplaced."

Vali shook his head, pressing his finger to his lips as though he could suppress the wave of indignation that rolled over him.

"Is that so, Seer?" Vali rose to his full height and faced the ancient one. "The gods have whispered their secrets in your ear?" His voice rose as frustration and bitterness threatened to overwhelm him.

"The gods' secrets are their own." Einar stood his ground, his voice unwavering.

He stopped in front of the Seer. "Then, what do you know of my anger?" Spittle flew with the vehemence of his question.

"You love her," said Einar. "But she is not yours to command."

Vali's ragged breath was like steam rising from a volcano.

"Men think they can command the Valkyrie, but they will learn in time they are wrong."

"Ragnar and the King may command her, but Brenna does not resist."

"Nei, do not think to know the mind of the Valkyrie."

"I know her better than most." Defiance bristled up Vali's spine.

"Mayhap," Einar bowed his head. "But you still have much to learn."

"I have no interest in learning the politics of land and kings," replied Vali, the words tasting bitter on his lips.

"What of destiny?"

The question caught Vali off guard. He stepped back, as if space would clarify the riddle. "My destiny is my own to determine."

"Ja, Styrimaðr."

Vali couldn't see the ancient one's eyes beneath the linen shroud. Still, he could feel them boring into him, rendering him momentarily speechless.

"And the Valkyrie's destiny is her own to choose."

He gave a slow nod. "She does not choose me."

"Stupid man," spat the Seer. "Your fate is entwined with

hers; the gods have determined this to be so. But until you understand her destiny, she will remain out of your reach."

Confusion clouded his mind. "You speak in riddles."

"I speak as the gods have bid me."

Vali turned, pacing back to the rock ledge. Fate and destiny. How was he to make sense of any of this? He'd never given much thought to his destiny, knowing only that he lived for the sea and the sword... and Brenna. What of her destiny? If he knew where her path would lead her, mayhap he would understand what the gods had in store for him. Twisting back to ask the Seer to speak plainly of Brenna and her destiny, he found an empty space where Einar had stood.

The Seer was gone, leaving Vali to his frustration. He drew in a lungful of the fresh mountain air, barely calming the steel edge of his nerves. The conversation with Einar had unravelled the momentary reprieve the climb had afforded him. His muscles began to groan their protest at the punishing regime he had inflicted on them. Yet, he could not stand on this mountain all day.

Sighing, he began the descent. Ignoring the view and thinking only of getting to the bottom, returning to the town and drowning his sorrows for the rest of the day in the alehouse.

22

*A*fter leaving Vali's tent, Brenna washed with a basin of water and changed her clothes. She sat long enough for Gita to brush her hair, explaining that if Vali was to come looking for her, the servant girl must send him away.

"You accepted the Jarl's proposal of marriage," Gita asked carefully.

"You heard the King's announcement."

"Ja, that is not what I asked."

The girl had been the closest thing Brenna had to a friend since her arrival in Birca. Despite the people's recent acceptance of her, there was no one else Brenna would call friend.

She sighed. "Oh, Gita. What choice do I have?"

"Naught," she'd agreed.

"Ja, if I accept Ubbe as my husband, mayhap he will keep his word and I will rule by his side."

"You do not love him?" Gita stopped the rhythmic stroke of the brush.

"Nei." She turned to face the girl. "Not many marry for love."

A tight smile appeared on Gita's face.

"What is it?" asked Brenna.

"There is talk," she began.

"Go on."

"Ubbe... he is not gentle in his ways with women."

Gita's eyes were firmly on her feet. Brenna thought back to her last conversation with Ubbe. He'd been quick to temper, his words revealing an ugly side. She swallowed her trepidation.

"I think it better not to pay any heed to idle chatter."

Gita nodded and returned to brushing Brenna's hair. She knew the girl had her best interests at heart, but she couldn't be dissuaded from her decision. She needed to put those thoughts from her mind. Besides, the casual rutting of a noble man with servants was hardly the same as sharing a marital bed. She hoped.

She wasted no more time, making her way directly to the great hall. Ubbe was seated upon the Jarl's chair, conferring with his men. Thankfully, Brenna couldn't see any sign of the

King or her father. Ubbe did not look up as she approached, although she'd seen another notice her arrival and whisper in his ear. Clearly, Ubbe's spies had done their job.

"I would speak with you, Jarl Ubbe." Her voice rose above the quiet rumble of discussion, causing most to pause to watch the spectacle unfold.

"I am busy." He did not even look up at her.

"I would prefer that we speak without an audience," she continued. "But if your work keeps you from attending to your future wife, I will say what I must, then leave you in peace."

Now he faced her. Molten fury burned through his eyes.

"Leave us," he roared.

The men at his side abruptly stood and made their way to the door. No one met her eyes as they filed past her. Servants scurried, hoping to avoid being caught in the eruption. Brenna raised her chin and stood her ground.

"You defied my command!" He pointed directly at her, as if there could be any confusion.

"I was not yours to command."

"You are to be my wife." He shortened the distance between them.

"I had not accepted." She did not flinch despite the rapid pace of her heart.

"You would defy the King and your father too?" His tone was low and menacing.

"I would enter this marriage of my own accord."

Ubbe almost choked on the laugh that escaped. "You think you have the right to choose?"

"I know I have the right to agree to this marriage and enter into it willingly, rather than under duress."

He stepped back, taking her measure. Brenna had not moved, still holding her head high as she waited for her words to sink in.

"You have decided you wish to marry me?"

She let the silence loom before speaking. "I will marry you Ubbe, but under the terms you offered me." She held up her hand to stop him from interrupting.

"I will marry you, and rule Birca by your side. Together."

Ubbe began to pace a slow circle around her.

"You wish to be my equal?"

"I wish to rule with you."

"But I am to be your husband and as such, I have the right to command you."

She bristled, thankful he could not see her face as he walked behind her. "If I am to be your wife and rule by your side, I would expect to be able to speak my mind on such matters pertaining to Birca."

His pacing had come full circle and he stood before her again.

"I would expect you would seek my counsel on matters pertaining to the rule of this land."

Ubbe grunted. "You expect a lot."

"I expect you to honour your word."

"When you do not honour yours?"

"If it is Vali you speak of, I gave no such assurance I would stay away from him."

Saying his name was like flame to kindle. Ubbe erupted in a rage.

"I will not be cuckolded by my own wife in front of the entire town." He stepped up so his face was an inch from her own.

"When I am your wife," she kept her voice firm and low. "I will not dishonour you in any way."

Ubbe squeezed her jaw in his hand. "Why should I believe you?" he spat.

"Because now I have agreed to this marriage."

His fingers pressed into her flesh so hard she thought he might dislocate her jaw. Yet, she did not recoil. Finally, he released her. Brenna clenched her hands into fists to stop herself from rubbing her face.

"Very well," he said. "I expect your willingness to be my wife to be evident to one and all from this moment forward."

Ubbe held her gaze, silently challenging her to defy him.

She smiled, hoping it reached her eyes. "As you wish."

Her stomach turned as he smirked at her.

"You are both here, good." Ragnar's booming voice brought their conversation to an end.

Ubbe brushed past her, all traces of anger gone. "Ragnar, I trust all the preparations for the wedding celebration are in hand?"

"Ja, everything is in order. I have brought my daughter an important gift."

Having composed herself once more, Brenna turned to face her father. Her mood lifted instantly.

"Mother?"

Hertha smiled as widely at Brenna, holding her arms open to receive her. "Daughter, are you well?"

Relief rushed through her body as she closed the gap between them. Happy tears pricked the back of her eyes.

"Ja, and you?"

They embraced, then held each at arm's length, both studying the face of the other. Her mother looked much as she always had. Her blonde hair sported more white strands in the elaborate braid, but her eyes sparkled as blue as the ocean, and her posture remained strong and regal. The months Brenna had been gone from her home faded away.

"I am all the better for seeing you, Mother."

"I could hardly let my daughter prepare for her marriage without me."

"I'm so grateful to have you here," she whispered against her ear, pulling her close again. Hertha had always been her sounding board, her voice of calm and reason. Her decision to marry Ubbe may be made, but she had much she wanted to discuss with her mother.

"Hertha, this is Ubbe, Jarl of Birca." Ragnar intervened.

Brenna had forgotten the man was still there. She stepped back to allow her mother to greet him.

"Jarl, it is an honour." Hertha bowed her head.

"The honour is all mine," said Ubbe. "Come, you must be hungry and thirsty after your journey."

Ubbe offered Hertha his arm. The servants, who had crept from their hiding places, set about bringing mead and bread and cheese for them to eat. Brenna took her place at the table, marvelling at the change in her future husband the moment her parents appeared. It seemed appearance was everything to Ubbe.

A fissure of dread crept into her heart as Gita's words of warning of Ubbe's less than gentle treatment of his bedmates fluttered in her memory.

AFTER THE MEAL, Ragnar and Ubbe excused themselves to attend to Aric, leaving Hertha and Brenna alone at last.

"Oh mother, I've missed you so much."

"I have missed you too, Daughter."

"There's so much I want to speak of."

Hertha smiled. "I hear the people of Birca have named you their Valkyrie?"

"Ja," Brenna chuckled. "It seems I have found my place here at last."

"Tarben was unkind?"

She sighed. "We were not well suited." She did not wish to speak ill of the late Jarl.

"And Ubbe?"

"Ubbe is... different to Tarben." What could she say? In truth, she did not know the man that was to be her husband at all well. Although she suspected he would not suffer the same affliction in the marital bed that Tarben had. Brenna could only hope he would keep his word and allow her to rule by his side.

Hertha rose, tucking her daughter's arm into hers. "We have plenty of time to talk. My women are erecting a tent for us to prepare you for your wedding tomorrow. You won't need to be anywhere except with me."

Brenna stopped, indignation flaring. "You mean you will be there to make sure I do not disappear with Vali."

Her mother gave her a tired smile. "Brenna-"

"You need not worry, mother. I have committed to this marriage."

"I am glad to hear it."

"Of course, I cannot speak for Vali. If he comes looking for me, just know I did not summon him."

Hertha patted her hand. "Oh, I do not believe we need to worry about that."

Remembering Ubbe's veiled threats, concern for the man whose tent she'd crept out of this morning froze her to the spot.

"What have they done to him?" she whispered.

"Nei, Daughter. It is what he has done to himself. Your father's men hauled him from an alehouse just before I arrived."

"Why? Where is he now?" Brenna may have chosen to marry Ubbe, but her heart still belonged to Vali. She could not stand to see him punished for being with her.

"Sleeping it off in his tent, I believe."

"Oh," she exhaled in relief.

No doubt he'd have a sore head come the morning. Mayhap it would keep him from witnessing her pledge herself to another man.

23

The tent Hertha's women had erected was a hive of activity. Her most trusted servants had travelled with her from Fornsigtuna, women who had been by her side since Hertha had first arrived, after her homeland had fallen to Gorm. They had known Brenna all her life and helped raise her alongside their own children.

The women of Birca also visited throughout the day. They wanted to ensure their Valkyrie had everything she needed for her impending wedding to their Jarl. They wanted to wish her well. Very soon the tent was full of wild flowers and plenty of food and mead.

Brenna had more than she needed and invited everyone to dine with them throughout the day and evening. The hours were filled with laughter and friendship, but left no time for Brenna to speak with Hertha about the burdens she carried in her heart.

Finally, as night fell, the women and children of Birca returned to their own homes. Hertha's women retired for the night and Brenna was at last alone with her mother. The fire pit and candle light offered a soft glow.

"The people here have come to love you, Brenna."

"They hold a special place in my heart as well."

"Ja, so I see." Hertha paused. "I wonder how much room is left in your heart for Ubbe?"

"You always could see right through me, Mother. It is true, the opportunity to care for these people has played a large role in my acceptance of this marriage."

Gita approached with a jug of mead. Hertha shook her head.

"Thank you Gita, that will be all. You should go and get some sleep," said Brenna. "Tomorrow will be a busy day."

Gita nodded, and withdrew.

"And Ubbe?"

Brenna frowned, her mother's question seemed to come from nowhere.

"How much of a role did Ubbe play in your decision to accept this marriage?"

Brenna examined her fingernails while she gathered her thoughts. "Ubbe is still a mystery to me." She chose a diplomatic response.

"Unlike Vali."

It was a statement, not a question. When she looked into her mother's eyes, she saw no pity or judgement, only kindness.

"Naught has changed since we last spoke of Vali," Brenna began.

"Naught? As in the kind of life he can offer you, or how you feel about him?"

"Both," she replied simply, too tired to hide the truth.

Hertha nodded. "I suspected as much."

She sighed. "Is it wrong that I put my ambitions above him?"

Her mother leaned in and covered her hands with her

own. "Nei, it is not your ambitions you are placing above him. It is Vali's desire for a different life than what you wish for yourself. You love him, I can see that. But is love enough?"

"Was love enough for you, mother?"

A wistful smile creased Hertha's features. "T'was more than love, daughter, that held me to your father's side. It was safety."

"I understand. By staying with father in Fornsigtuna, you were no threat to Gorm and your family's rightful throne."

"Ja, that is true. But by staying with Ragnar, I kept my people safe. I could not bear for more blood to be spilled."

"You were protecting your people," whispered Brenna, comprehension unlocking some of the questions she'd always had about her mother's inaction to claim the throne.

Hertha reached up and stroked Brenna's cheek. She leant into the caress, savouring her mother's touch.

"I think, mayhap, we are not that dissimilar," her mother said.

Brenna shook her head. "When men go to war, their thoughts are on battle and strategy. The welfare of their women and children, of the older ones, is not a consideration."

She knew when her people raided on foreign shores, they killed all who crossed their path. That often included women and children. It was not so different when Vikings attacked each other. Women and children were expected to take up weapons and fight. Or find somewhere to hide. No thought was given to ensuring their safety as part of the battle strategy. At least, not that she'd witnessed in Fornsigtuna or Birca.

"I can fight as well as any warrior, but I can protect these people in other ways as well. I want to protect all of Birca, and watch the settlement grow and thrive."

Hertha squeezed her daughter's hand. "We are not dissimilar at all."

Brenna felt her heart grow warm. She had never been able to articulate this to anyone else. Mayhap, not even herself until recently. Her ambition to rule was not about personal power, it was a desire to serve and to protect. To lead by example and unite her people, rather than conquer them.

"Love eventually came," said Hertha, breaking Brenna from her own thoughts. She shook her head, not understanding her mother's meaning.

"With Ragnar," she smiled. "I was grateful, of course. He saved me from Gorm and a fate far worse than death. But I did not love him."

Brenna stilled. She had always believed her parents married for love.

"I married your father because he offered me safety. He offered my people safety." She looked off into the distance. "Ragnar is an incredible man. Capable of great feats of bravery on the battlefield, but also of such kindness and tenderness. Eventually, I grew to love him."

"Do you think that's possible for Ubbe and I?" whispered Brenna.

Her mother smiled. "Anything is possible."

24

*T*he following morning dawned bright and beautiful. The sky was a vibrant blue without a cloud in sight.

"Frigga approves of this marriage. Look at the day she has given you!"

As was the custom for weddings, it was Friday, Frigga's day. The women busied themselves drawing a bath for Brenna, telling stories of Odin's own wedding to Frigga, the goddess of love and marriage. Brenna tried to ignore the sense of unease in her belly, focusing on the stories and the rituals rather than the vows she was about to take.

Once she was bathed and clean, Hertha presented Brenna with a simple gown of soft green fabric that clung to her hips and breasts, accentuating her shapely body.

The women set about binding her hair, an elaborate work of art that took more than an hour of careful braiding. A crown of silver was placed on her head, the same crown her mother had worn to wed Ragnar. The same crown she had worn when she married Tarben.

This time, the women created a beautiful garland of

wildflowers to surround the crown, and the braids were much more intricate than she'd worn for her first marriage. The finished creation was fitting of a Valkyrie on her wedding day.

"You are beautiful, my Daughter," said Hertha, her eyes shining with unshed tears.

"Thank you, Mother."

"It is time."

In the distance, they could hear the musicians playing. Melodies created by cow horns and lyres played in time with the drums. Brenna walked with her mother, surrounded by women from both Fornsigtuna and Birca. She couldn't help but smile as people called out blessings and well wishes, hailing her their Valkyrie. Brenna could not deny that Birca was her home and these people were her family now. She focused only on those around her, refusing to lift her gaze beyond the joyful faces in her direct line of sight. Refusing to acknowledge the growing doubt in her heart.

They reached a clearing where Ubbe stood waiting for her. His hair was freshly washed and braided; a beautiful leather chest piece covered his white shirt. He wore his great, black fur that made his broad shoulders seem even bigger. The smile on his face lit up his eyes. He reminded Brenna of the man who promised to honour her as his equal and have her rule by his side. Mayhap her mother was right, and love would come eventually.

So why did she feel so wretched? She'd decided to let go of Vali, but her heart would not concede.

Ubbe reached for her hand and she grasped it, if only to distract herself from the tears that threatened. She would comply with their agreement. Birca would see her happily wed to their Jarl. She looked up at her groom, and smiled.

Hertha joined her husband and the King. A priest from Uppsala had come to perform the wedding ritual. A blackened strip ran across both eyes and around his shaved head. He wore a simple white tunic, belted at his waist with a gold cord.

"Today we bear witness to the joining of this man and this woman before the gods," he began.

Before the gods, thought Brenna. The gods who watch me, who see me. Do they see through me?

The crowd parted and a goat was led in to stand before a small cauldron. The priest took the knife offered and held it beneath the throat of the goat.

"We offer this sacrifice to the mighty Thor," he said as he slid the knife across the animal's flesh. "And ask him to bless the union of Jarl Ubbe and Brenna of Birca with strength and courage."

The goat fell to its knees, its head held over the cauldron as its blood filled the vessel. The priest took the cauldron and placed it on top of a pile of rocks. A small altar had been set up with wood carvings of the gods - Odin, Frigga, Thor, Freyr and Loki. The priest scooped the blood in his hand and drizzled it over the carvings, before turning to Brenna and Ubbe and marking their foreheads, and his own, with the same blood. He took a twig and thrust it into the blood.

"With this sacrifice," the priest began to fling the blood on those assembled, starting with King Aric, Ragnar and Hertha, "we witness the joining of gods and people."

Ubbe reached across and ran his thumb across Brenna's brow, stemming the tiny trickles of blood from reaching her eyes.

"I believe the gods are with us today."

She smiled back at him. "Ja, the gods have fated this day."

Please, let it be so.

The priest returned to them and clasped his hands over theirs.

"May Odin give them knowledge on their way to come, may Frigga bless them with love, may Thor bless their union with strength and courage, may Freyr bless them with many sons and prosperity, may Loki never deny them laughter."

"Ubbe, do you swear before the gods on this day that you want to take this woman as your wife?"

"I swear by Odin and Frigga." Ubbe never took his eyes from hers.

"Brenna, do you swear before the gods on this day that you want to take this man as your husband?"

"I swear by Odin and Frigga," her voice was strong, as if it belonged to someone else.

One of Ubbe's warriors stepped forward, placing a sword across his outstretched hands. On the hilt, he placed a small ring made of gold.

"Brenna, I give you this sword - my father's sword - for you to keep until our eldest son is strong enough to lift it."

He placed the sword in her hands. The metal was heavy and cool, the hilt was well-worn. Ubbe took the ring and she gave the sword to her mother to hold. Turning to face her groom, she held her hand steady between them, drawing in a deep breath to keep the tremor at bay.

"With this ring," he began to slide it onto her finger. "I bind you to me, as my wife."

He raised her hand to his lips, placing a gentle kiss upon the ring.

Ragnar stepped forward, with the sword of his own father. She recognised the bronze sword with the ornate handle as the same one she'd given Tarben on their wedding day. Ragnar must have retrieved it from their bedchamber. She had not given it a second thought. As her father placed it across her hands, adding a ring of gold to the hilt, Brenna found her mind drifting from the ceremony.

Was Vali here? Was he watching this take place?

Brenna cleared her throat and raised her chin. She could not let Vali intrude. She must focus.

"Ubbe, I give you this sword - my grandfather's sword - as a symbol of the joining of our two families as one."

She placed the sword into Ubbe's waiting hands and took the ring, holding on to it as Ubbe handed the weapon to the warrior waiting behind him. He turned back to her, the smile on his face unchanged. It seemed he'd not noticed her momentary falter.

"With this ring," she took Ubbe's hand in her own and pushed the ring upward, "I bind you to me." She swallowed the rising lump in her throat and forced herself to look up at him. "As my husband."

She sent a silent prayer to Frigga that love for her new husband would come eventually, and her love for Vali would fade, as would his for her. Surely the gods would grant her that small mercy.

"Allfather, Odin his holy name. Ragnarok will come, his destiny must be fulfilled. On earth and in Asgard may Odin's will guide us." The priest stepped closer to Brenna and Ubbe.

"Father of everything, allow our swords to strike accurate. Make our arms stronger than anyone who wants to destroy us."

"By destiny, Ubbe and Brenna are aligned, their love eternal and true. May they face their challenges together and find strength in their union. By the sun, moon and stars, this marriage is blessed by the gods."

A cheer erupted from the crowd. It was done. They were married. Before another thought could form, Ubbe pressed his lips to hers, his tongue probing her lips and clenched teeth. She stiffened, an involuntary reaction she could not control. She may have agreed to this marriage, but it seemed her body was yet to feel the same.

Ubbe drew back, all trace of his smile gone from his eyes. "You are my wife and I will have you tonight," he growled into her ear, his hands pulling her hips roughly against him. "Whether you agree to it or not."

25

A combination of the light and his own sour breath roused him. Vali was lying face down on his furs, the bitter aftertaste of beer assailing him. He groaned and attempted to roll over, landing on the ground heavily on his side. His body was content to remain where he was, but his throat screamed for water. Clawing his way into a sitting position, the full effect of yesterday's drinking session slammed into his skull.

"By the gods..."

Movement activated the acid roiling in his belly. It rose at a rapid pace. On hands and knees, Vali crawled to the entrance of the tent, and barely managed to poke his head out before his guts expelled their contents in convulsive waves.

Swiping his hand across his mouth, he squinted around, the sun burning his eyes. The tents and paths around them appeared to be deserted. Backing himself into the tent, he sat back. His head throbbed mercilessly. It seemed to be keeping time with something, a distant beat. Scrubbing his hands over his face, he reached for the kernel of a thought that was rattling around his brain.

Today was Brenna's wedding day.

The hammer crushing his skull from the inside must be keeping time with the wedding musicians. A low whine escaped, representing the amount of pain in his head, and his heart.

He shuffled over to the basin of water and scooped the lukewarm liquid over his face and into his mouth. What he really needed was to submerge his body in the cool water of the fjord. He glanced down at himself. He was still wearing the clothes he had on yesterday. The beer had seeped through his skin and even Vali couldn't stand the smell. He started unlacing his boots, prolonging the time before he would need to stand.

He wiggled his bare toes, the only part of him that didn't smell of stale beer. Leaning onto his hands and knees again, he used the centre pole to steady himself as he staggered to his feet. When the tent stopped spinning and the ground beneath his feet evened out, he took a few tentative steps on his own. Satisfied he could walk, he pushed upon the flaps and stepped out into the blazing sunlight.

Vali started towards the fjord, his progress stilted as he battled the sun and his hangover. A servant girl appeared before him. The look of disgust on her face confirmed he looked as bad as he felt.

After several torturous minutes, he reached the banks of the fjord. A few fishermen were cleaning their nets, elbowing each other and nodding in Vali's direction. Ignoring their jibes, he lifted his tunic and with a few tugs, freed himself from the soiled garment, enjoying the instant relief brought by the cool air on his skin. He stepped free of his trousers and walked straight into the water.

The icy freshness was instantly reviving. Vali sank down into the depths, pleased to be transported from his reality for a few moments. Coming back up for air, he swam away from the bank. He flipped over onto his back and let himself float.

The light still hurt his eyes but the thudding in his skull had been shocked into a low roar. The sky was a brilliant blue, without a single cloud. Little chance of Thor appearing to bring his strength and courage for Vali to face the day and everything it meant. He closed his eyes and relished the feeling of freedom as his body drifted.

Vali remembered little from the previous day after he'd been at the alehouse for an hour or so. He'd handed over a small fortune in silver and told the serving girl to keep the beer coming. Somehow, he'd made his way back to his tent. It was possible he got there under his own steam, but chances were, he'd had some help. Judging from the state of him, he'd not had any female company.

"More's the pity..." he murmured out loud, even though he knew he didn't really mean it. He'd drowned his sorrows because he had no interest in trying to distract himself with other pleasures.

At least he hadn't gotten himself into any major trouble. He'd no doubt Ragnar and Aric would welcome an excuse to have him locked up and out of the way.

His stomach rumbled, hunger creeping up on him. Thank the gods, he'd not drifted too far from the shore. Turning in its direction, he swam a steady stroke until his feet found the bottom. He hadn't thought to bring a fresh change of clothes with him - he hadn't thought of anything except getting to the water. One sniff of the clothes he'd left on the sandy bank almost turned his stomach. There was nothing for it, he would walk back to his tent naked.

The sun warmed his skin as he strode back through the makeshift tents. He encountered the same serving girl he'd seen on the way to the fjord. This time her eyes were so wide they nearly fell out of her head.

He chuckled to himself, imagining she thought him completely mad. Or mayhap she'd reconsidered him after witnessing his... muscular build.

He found some fresh clothes and dressed. His hunger had only grown since leaving the water. The last thing he wanted to do was take any part in the celebration of Brenna marrying another man - again. But as everyone in town would be at the feast, the chances of coming face to face with Ubbe, Ragnar, Aric, or worse, Brenna, was minimal. He hoped.

To HIS RELIEF, the wedding was well and truly over by the time he reached the marketplace. It was bustling with people, not working but making their way to the great hall and surrounding area, where food and beer would flow freely for one and all. Roasting meat permeated the air, calling to his growling stomach. Joy abounded like an insidious disease. One man actually slapped him on the back and encouraged him to praise the gods at such a wondrous match as Brenna and Ubbe. Everyone was in high spirits. Irritation grated with every step he took.

Birca would get to keep their Valkyrie. He didn't begrudge the people that. They didn't know their underhanded King had taken the woman he loved from him not once, but twice. That her father had orchestrated the deal. That she had chosen them over him. He refused to believe she'd chosen Ubbe over him. This was about her damned ambition.

The frustration he'd managed to drown with beer yesterday came rushing back and he mumbled a curse, invoking Loki as the instigator of his troubles. He picked up his pace towards the tables set up outside the hall; he just wanted to eat his fill and drink enough beer to make him forget what it was in honour of. This time, he would drink at the expense of those who would deny him his destiny.

He cared little for the people meandering towards the feast, barging his way through without apology. He ignored the shouts of reprimand, turning to glare at one man who threatened to teach him some manners. The threat was quickly withdrawn.

Turning back, he collided with another group of revellers, sending a woman sprawling onto her knees.

"You there!" boomed a familiar voice.

Vali whirled around to face King Aric, whose face distorted with anger even further when he recognised the culprit.

"Vali Hrolfsson."

Vali heard the derision in his voice and plastered a smirk across his face. "King Aric."

"You're in a hurry."

"Of course," his contempt took over. "I want to be the first to give my well wishes to the happy couple."

"You'll stay away from Brenna," growled the King.

"Why? I have no claim to her, you made sure of that, Aric. You've married her off." He threw his arms wide. "Again."

"By the gods-"

"Arrest him!" Ragnar interrupted the King.

"The father of the bride," Vali raised his voice. "What a joyful day this is for you."

Huscarls surrounded him, holding him by his arms and

forcing him to his knees.

"Oh, Vali."

Vali looked up into the disappointed face of Hertha. "Come to watch your daughter be sold off again?"

The blunt handle of a spear landed in his guts, knocking the wind from him.

"Get him out of my sight," glowered the King. "Lock him up!"

Vali barely had his breath back when the huscarls began dragging him through the crowd. "I can walk."

His words were swallowed by the boos and jeers of the crowd. He tried to bring his feet up beneath him, only to find the handle of the spear between his shoulder blades, knocking him to his knees again.

After a few minutes, the huscarls grew tired of dragging him through the village and dumped him on his face in the ground.

"Get on your feet, dunga!"

He spat the dirt from his mouth, then lifted himself off the ground, choosing to keep the smart response to himself. They grabbed him by the shoulders and pushed him forward. He was marched to the outskirts of the town, to the enclosures reserved for animals.

The huscarls pushed him through a wooden door and his nose was instantly assaulted with the sharp smell of recently excreted onions and carrots.

"You couldn't find a stable with a rotting corpse to cover the smell of the pig shit?"

Without a word from his captors, his hands were bound and the end of the rope secured to a steel pole protruding from the ground. He heard the beam of wood slide into place and block the door from the outside. Sighing, he leant his back against the wall and slid to the ground.

26

With the ceremony over, it was time for the feast. Ubbe walked ahead and was waiting at the entrance to the great hall. Brenna suppressed a groan. Even Tarben had not bothered to carry her into the hall on their wedding day, and there was little chance she'd trip over the threshold she'd entered hundreds of times.

Still, Ubbe wasn't going to be deterred by the pained expression she wore, so she allowed him to hoist her into his arms amidst the cheers of well-wishers, and carry her inside. Feeling more like a prized pig than a cherished bride, she forced a smile for the benefit of the crowd.

Her return to the ground was equally as abrupt. Gita appeared at her side to steady her as Ubbe was busy unsheathing his sword.

"Stand back," he announced.

He widened his stance and pointed the sword at the ceiling, playing up the drama of lining up his target. With an almighty heft, the sword flew into the air, sticking fast into the ceiling. Another cheer erupted and Ubbe walked a slow circle, accepting the accolades of his peers.

"See that, Wife?" He turned back to Brenna. "We will be together until Valhalla calls."

"Till death do we part." She plastered another smile across her face.

"Come, let the feast begin," Ubbe took her by the elbow to lead her to the main table.

"Where is the King and your parents?" he hissed.

She tried to peer behind him, only to be twisted back in the direction they were walking. "How should I know?"

They reached the long table atop the dais. Wildflowers that matched those in her crown sat along its length facing the room. Under any other circumstances she'd have thought the arrangement beautiful. Instead, she felt suffocated by their gentle fragrance.

"The King needs to give the first toast," he growled.

"I'm sure they will not be far away."

Ubbe pulled out the high-backed chair and she sat, smoothing her skirt beneath her. He pushed the chair in from behind and leaned over, his hot breath pressed against her neck.

"I like the view from up here, Wife." It took all her willpower not to shudder. "I look forward to having my way with you later this night."

Revulsion fluttered in her belly. She prayed to Loki her new husband would continue to stick with tradition and drink the bridal-ale until he was incapable of consummating the marriage.

People continued to enter the great hall, filling the tables and sucking all the air from the room. Brenna tried to concentrate on looking serene but her mind was racing. Gita's words of warning rang in her ears. Could she avoid her marital duties tonight – but to what end? Ubbe was her husband now and she could not deny him. Mayhap it was better to get it over with while her mother was still in Birca. If Ubbe was terribly cruel, mayhap her parents would demand he release her. Which raised the questions, where were her parents and the King?

A flurry of activity at the entrance came in answer. The King and his entourage, including Ragnar and Hertha, came through the door. People rose and shouted their blessings to the gods for the King's health. Ubbe and Brenna stood as they made their way to the main table. Brenna accepted her mother's kiss on her cheek and acknowledged her father's hand on her shoulder.

Horns of mead and beer appeared and King Aric remained standing, waiting for the crowd to quieten.

"Anyone would think it was his wedding," grumbled Ubbe beside her.

"I thought you were waiting upon his arrival for this precise moment," she said through her forced grin.

"Here we are, celebrating the joining of Jarl Ubbe and the Valkyrie of Birca." Aric's voice travelled across the heads of all gathered in the hall. "We drink to their health and happiness, and to the wealth and prosperity of Birca! Skal!"

"Skal!"

The response reverberated around the hall.

The musicians began to play and servants entered with platters laden with meat and vegetables. Laughter and light-hearted banter resounded, and Brenna felt herself relax a little.

Brenna surveyed the meat on offer; it looked delicious but her stomach reeled against the idea of food.

"Eat, you'll need your energy for later, Wife," Ubbe drawled in her ear.

Acid churned in her belly. She selected some chicken and nodded her thanks to the serving girl. Conversation flowed around her while Brenna pushed her food around her plate, taking a small bite here and there. More to keep her mouth and hands busy and avoid talking to her husband. Ubbe was in his element, speaking much louder than was necessary as the King and her father spoke of their recent battles and future plans for Birca.

Her eyes roamed the hall, taking in the merriment around her. She was glad to be able to grant her people this feast and a sense of hope that their future looked bright. At the touch of her elbow, she leaned her head towards her mother.

"He's not here," Hertha whispered.

Brenna turned to look at her; eyebrows raised in question.

Hertha frowned. "Vali."

"I wasn't looking for him."

Her mother inhaled sharply, as though swallowing whatever retort had sat on her tongue. In truth, Brenna had put Vali out of head. She couldn't marry Ubbe while thinking of him. If she allowed Vali to enter her thoughts, her heart would ache too much and test her resolve in a manner she may not be able to withstand. She hoped he would stay away, for her sake as much as his.

"It is time for you to serve the bridal-ale," her mother said.

"Ah..."

Another tradition Ubbe was no doubt looking forward to. Hertha signalled to Gita to bring the ale horn. Brenna rose from her chair. Ubbe gave her a questioning stare. She replied with a smile, touching his shoulder lightly. Most of the people in the hall were watching and she was resigned to playing her role.

Taking the ale horn from Gita, she gifted her husband a

coy smile. He returned in kind, settling back in his chair as Brenna made her way to the barrel of honey-based mead that had been brought from Fornsigtuna as the bridal ale. The barrel contained enough ale for Ubbe and Brenna to drink from every night for the next month, as tradition dictated.

Brenna filled the horn and returned to the table. Holding the vessel aloft, she began to speak.

"Before us, we have this. Honey and mead. The drink of the gods!"

The crowd roared their agreement.

"We drink from this horn in the hope we will drink from the vast well of knowledge held by the Allfather."

She turned to Ubbe. Amusement danced in his eyes.

"I hallow this horn of mead, to the gods and goddesses, the Odin and Frigga, to Thor and Sit, Freya and Freyr. I ask you to bless this wedding. Bless my husband."

She raised her horn higher. "Skal."

"Skal," returned the people.

She held the horn to Ubbe's lips, tilting it until the mead trickled down his chin. He jumped to his feet and wrapped his arms around her waist, lifting her off her feet. He planted his lips firmly on hers, the taste of mead strong. The crowd continued to cheer.

Taking the horn from her hands, he made the sign of a hammer over it, in honour of Thor.

"We drink to Odin, Frigga and Thor. Bless this union, and bless my wife. May she give me many strong sons. Skal!"

He brought the horn to her mouth. She swallowed the dregs of the mead and tried not to grimace outwardly as Ubbe kissed her again.

"More mead," he called.

The musicians struck another merry tune and the celebration continued. Brenna settled back into her chair, her horn of mead in her hand. She had no intention of honouring the tradition of getting drunk with her husband on her wedding night. But to anyone watching, she would always have her drink in hand.

Tables were pulled back for dancing. Warriors challenged each other to wrestling bouts over good natured insults. Brenna and her mother stayed at the table. She only had this night left with Hertha and she wanted to make the most of her mother's company. The smile on her face and the joy in her eyes was genuine as she listened to the stories being told by her mother and the other women.

Whatever the cost, Brenna had chosen this life, and she was determined to make the best of it.

27

*T*he wedding feast was a distant rumble that insisted on intruding on Vali's thoughts. Many months at sea had given him the ability to occupy his mind when there was naught to do, yet tonight he was unable to keep his focus on anything else for more than a minute.

Bitterness looked to have won out over hurt, despair, anger and indifference. Until self-pity trumped them all. Despite his protestations to the contrary, Vali knew he had naught to blame but himself for his current predicament. Hel, mayhap it was his fault Brenna did not choose him.

A voice in his head started to argue her lack of choice, but he waved the notion away. He'd gone around and around all of this and he was tired riding the whirlpool. It had landed him in this stinking pig pen, with his stomach rumbling despite the acrid aroma, and a thirst for more beer to help him forget.

"By the gods, I'm surprised you're not dead from the smell."

The door cracked open, emitting a warm glow from distant fires and the form of Frode.

"I hope you've brought food as well as your wit," Vali said.

"Are you sure you can stomach it?" Frode produced a portion of bread and roasted chicken wrapped in cloth. Vali reached for the offering as Frode crouched beside him, wrinkling his nose at the stench.

"Shall I cut your bindings?"

"Nei, I've no time for you to saw through this rope. I need food more than freedom at this moment."

Vali tore in the meat, almost too fast to savour the taste.

"When did you last eat?"

He shrugged. "Yesterday."

"I fear you are turning into a pig the way you are taking to your food."

Vali snorted, his mouth too full to reply.

"So, once your stomach is full, am I freeing you? I can make ready the boat. Most of the guards are too drunk to pay much mind."

Vali regarded his friend in the shadowed light. Frode had already risked much by bringing him food. The King would have him flogged if he was caught, or worse.

"They would know who helped me. I will face the King alone."

"You wouldn't have to face him at all if you came with me now."

"Ja, but what of next week, and the week after?" Vali stared into the face of his closest friend, grateful for his loyalty. " I won't keep you from your home and I won't be kept from mine. Aric would catch up with me eventually. I'd rather have it said and done sooner than later."

Frode stood and Vali could barely make out Frode's features, but he imagined him widening his eyes as if to say 'I did offer.'

"I don't suppose you brought me anything to drink?"

Frode loosened the leather pouch hanging from his belt, passing it to Vali. "It's only water."

Vali downed the contents of the pouch before handing it back. "Thank you, Frode. But you should get out of here in case the guards come to check on me."

"*I* will come to check on you before I turn in for the night."

Laughter rose above the music outside. Vali gritted his teeth and willed himself not to ask. He lost the battle. "The wedding feast goes well then?"

Frode exhaled. "Brenna stays with her mother and her women. She seems content."

Vali nodded to himself. "And the groom?"

"Drunk."

"And pleased with himself," Vali mumbled.

"Vali-"

"Don't worry yourself, Frode. As long as Brenna is happy..." He couldn't bring himself to finish the sentiment. He doubted anything would make him happy right now.

28

*H*ertha leaned toward her daughter. "I believe we shall say goodnight now."

Brenna looked at her mother, unsure of her meaning. Hertha nodded behind her at the merry band of drunken guests - three men from the council and their wives - who had gathered to escort the bride and groom to their sleeping chamber. Inwardly, she shuddered at the bawdy banter between the rowdy group and her very drunk husband about what the next part of his evening would entail.

She faced her mother again. "I shall bid you goodnight before I am summoned."

"A wise idea," agreed Hertha.

The women rose with Brenna. She kissed her mother, then gathered her dignity and moved towards her husband and the party who were charged with bearing witness to the final ritual of the wedding night. Although, she sincerely hoped they would not be staying once they reached the chamber door.

"Wife! We are to bed!"

Brenna regarded Ubbe's glassy eyes, noting he was still

standing on his own two feet. She had no idea what his current state meant for consummating their marriage. Regardless, she hoped his memory would fail him and she would not need to participate beyond the perfunctory requirements. She gave him a smile and took his proffered arm.

The musicians started a high-spirited tune, inciting the wedding guests to rise to their feet to clap and cheer the Jarl and his Valkyrie on.

"Stay and drink!" called Ubbe. "Make merry with each other!"

They left the great hall and wound their way through the outside revellers, accepting their toasts and well wishes. The King was still ensconced in the private quarters of the great hall and a bridal couch had been prepared in the tent previously used for Brenna's preparations with her women. It was a further walk in the night air, which would have been pleasant except it appeared to be having a sobering effect on her husband.

Once they were clear of the feast, Ubbe pulled her hard against his side. "I'm looking forward to having what is mine."

Brenna had no intention of making the experience any less pleasant than it needed to be so she smiled up at her husband, despite the hard glint in his eye. He grunted his approval, relaxing his grip a little.

The path to the bridal tent was lit with torches. The sound of the wedding feast behind them masked the noises of the night. Most of the villagers had attended the feast, however it seemed strange to encounter no other soul the further they moved away. Mayhap Ubbe and his guard had warned the people earlier to stay well clear of the newly-weds and their sleeping quarters. If he anticipated any resistance from his new bride, Ubbe would not want his people to know the marriage was anything less than a happy union. She pushed the prickle of unease aside.

The sound of speed cutting through the air alerted Brenna to trouble a second before the arrows hit their marks, and four of their six escorts fell. So accurate, they were dead before they hit the ground. Brenna reached for her dagger by instinct, the sting of fear filling the spot it usually occupied. They were unarmed, all of them.

She looked to take cover, but there was none to be had without chancing the danger lurking in the shadows. A scream was cut short. Brenna spun around in time to see the light leave the woman's eyes, blood spilling from her slit throat. Her killer released his hold, letting her crumple to the ground.

The air grew heavy as the remaining three were surrounded. Men clad in dark clothes crowded the group. The last of their escorts flailed for a moment at the strong arms that encircled his head and shoulders, then the dagger sliced his throat and ended his struggle.

Ubbe and Brenna stood back to back, their fighting instincts taking over.

"Who are you?" he demanded. "What do you want?"

A figure stepped out of the darkness, Brenna and Ubbe turned as one to face him. Dressed in black trousers and tunic, and leather armour, the man stood eye to eye with Ubbe. Clearly, he was the leader of this attack.

"What do I want?" His voice was low and mean. "Not much. Just your title, your lands and your wife."

"Odin will strike-"

In one fluid movement he pulled the axe from his side, stepped back and brought the weapon down onto Ubbe's skull. His warm blood spattered across Brenna's face, and that of his killer. She clenched her fists and refused to flinch - to feel anything for the man she'd just wed - keeping her focus on the man who'd just murdered him.

"Despite the stories, I am not a god," he said. "*Sigurd* struck you down."

"Sigurd the Black," whispered Brenna.

"Ja, Valkyrie." He stepped closer, his face an inch from her own. "I am Sigurd the Black."

She took in his dark blue eyes, a scar running from above his left eye to his cheek. In the fire light, she saw touches of brown in his black beard and hair, half tied back so its length fell over his shoulders. He was as tall as Ubbe, but much broader across the shoulders.

"No doubt you've heard of me?"

Her need to survive cowered behind her warrior instincts as outrage swept over her.

"I have battled your forces - and won - twice over. Yet this is the first time I have lain eyes on you. Are you afraid to face the full might of Birca?"

He held her gaze for a moment before unleashing a belly laugh. What kind of man was this? His men joined him in his mirth until he silenced them by bringing his axe to Brenna's throat. The blade was wet with Ubbe's blood.

"You might find a little more respect for me, Valkyrie."

"I have no respect for a man who would kill a warrior without a blade in his hand."

Sigurd shrugged. "Jarl Ubbe will not feast in the great hall of Valhalla for all eternity. I doubt Odin will miss him too much."

Brenna strained her ears against the night. Surely someone would come down this path soon. Mayhap the King and her father had already been alerted to Sigurd's presence. She just needed to keep the brute talking a little longer.

"What do you know of Jarl Ubbe and his skill on the battlefield?"

"I know it was not either of the jarls who led Birca to victory."

The sharp edge of the axe bit against her skin, yet she stood her ground. If Sigurd had wanted her dead, she would not be breathing.

"What do you want from me?"

An ugly smirk appeared on his face.

"Everything."

The pressure of the blade against her neck disappeared, and then the world turned black.

29

The feast continued outside his prison. Laughter and voices shouting to be heard over the musicians. Only moments ago, Vali had listened to the crowd cheering the newlyweds on their way to the bridal couch. He'd nearly brought the chicken and bread back up at the thought of Ubbe touching Brenna. By the gods, what he wouldn't give to drown his sorrows right now. Anything to not have to think about Brenna, and what she was doing. To not have to think at all. Or feel.

Mayhap this pig stye suited him and his melancholy. It was the only place in the village that was not a scene of drunken merriment. No amount of alcohol could make bearing witness to Ubbe carrying his new wife off to bed palatable. Vali stretched his spine, then settled back against the wall and his misery. What did it matter if he allowed himself to wallow? It seemed the most appropriate course of action.

Muffled shouts broke through his reverie. A fight between drunken louts, no doubt. He didn't bother lifting his gaze from the mud. When the music ceased, midway through the tune, Vali returned his senses to the outside world. The musicians would not stop playing for a fight amongst the villagers. Something more serious had occurred.

The shouting was distorted. Women screamed. Were they under attack once more? He struggled against his bindings. If Sigurd had come back, he'd chosen an opportune moment. Most of the warriors and townsfolk would be drunk and unarmed. The small guard would be easily overrun by a greater force, especially this late in the evening. He needed to get out. He needed to see what was going on.

Pulling against the ropes only tightened them. He tried to loosen them with his teeth, spitting out the mud and shit that had caked itself into the knot. Desperate, he searched the shadows for something to grind the rope against. When that failed, he focused his efforts on trying to pull the iron peg attached to the rope, from the ground. He pushed the peg back and forth, hoping to detach it from the earth.

After several minutes of effort, Vali had forced a little movement. The mud was soft but the dirt beneath was packed solid; the peg hammered in deep. He wasn't going to sit here while the town burned and its people were slaughtered. While Brenna may be in danger. He kept rocking the peg back and forth, side to side. Sweat stung his eyes and his hands blistered and bled, but he did not stop. The yelling and screaming continued. Footsteps pounded past his prison.

He paused. Not horses; human. Nor could he detect the sound of sword or axe on shield and flesh. Sniffing the air, the telltale waft of burning thatch was absent. Yet something was wrong. He pushed at the peg with even greater force.

The door behind him burst open, slamming against the wall.

"Frode! What kept-"

Vali wiped the sweat from his eyes. It was not Frode.

"Get up," growled Ragnar. His wild eyes and the glint of his dagger flashed in the darkened space.

He pushed up off his knees. If Ragnar was going to use the cover of whatever chaos was taking place outside to kill him, he would stand and demand his opportunity to enter Valhalla.

"You would kill an unarmed warrior?"

"Nei," Ragnar grunted, grasping Vali's forearm and sawing at the rope.

What in Hel was going on? The chaos of whatever lay outside continued. Vali glanced at the open door but saw no sign of any other of the huscarl.

"Ragnar, what is happening? Is it Sigurd?"

"Ja."

The ropes fell to the ground. Vali rubbed at his wrists to bring the circulation back. "His army attacks the town again?"

The older man shook his head

His patience was at an end. "Ragnar!"

Vali noticed the panic in his eyes and for the first time in his whole life, Ragnar looked small beneath his fur. "Brenna?"

"A small party was escorting Brenna and Ubbe to their bridal chambers when they were attacked," began Ragnar.

"Was it the huscarl of Ubbe's guard escorting them?"

Ragnar shook his head. "Neither. They were unarmed."

Vali hissed his disapproval.

"Ubbe insisted. He'd also made sure the townspeople were kept well clear of their path."

"How did they defend themselves?"

"They didn't. Not that it would've mattered. Sigurd's

archers felled four of the party, the other two had their throats slit. Ubbe is also dead."

All of the oxygen dissipated and Vali struggled to draw air into his lungs. "Brenna?"

Ragnar looked him in the eye for the first time since freeing him. Fear replaced his usual steely stare. "She's gone."

His heart leapt into his throat. How was this possible?

"Gone?" Vali stepped forward, the action bringing his senses back. "Mayhap she got away and is hiding?"

"The town is being searched. It makes no sense to remain hidden."

"You said it was Sigurd, but how do you know? Brenna may stay hidden if she feels the threat is from within Birca."

"A slave almost stumbled into the middle of the attack. She was afraid Ubbe would have her thrashed and stayed hidden. She realised too late what was happening but heard Sigurd identify himself."

"The slave saw Sigurd take Brenna?"

"Ja. She thought Sigurd had killed Brenna when he hit her with the back of his axe. But he carried her away."

"That explains why she did not fight him."

"Aric is assembling his men."

Realisation began to dawn. "Are they fit to fight, to travel?"

"Barely."

Hurried footsteps sounded at the door a second before Frode appeared.

"What took you?" spat Ragnar.

Frode's arms were laden. "If you'll recall, all Hel has broken loose." He turned to Vali. "I have clean clothes, your boots and your shield and weapons."

He held them out to Ragnar rather than Vali. Detaching the pouch from his belt, he threw it to his Styrimaðr.

Vali nodded and took a long draught from the pouch. He changed from his stinking tunic and trousers into the fresh linens, pulling his leather vest over his head as Ragnar explained his men found evidence of a boat that had been beached on the other side of the town.

"Where has he taken her?"

"If it were me," said Ragnar. "I would return to my stronghold where I can best defend against an attack."

"Tingvalla in Karlstad."

"Ja, he took Tingvalla after starving the people out. Those he hadn't killed in raids. Most of the surrounding villages have fallen, or capitulated, to Sigurd's rule."

"Yet he's made no claim on Karlstad itself?" mused Vali, sliding his sword into his back scabbard.

"It makes no sense," agreed Frode. "He craves land and power by all accounts."

"Yet he wastes his time and men on attacking Birca," said Vali.

"And now he's taken my daughter."

"He's taken the Fru of Birca. The woman has outlived the last two Jarls."

"You think he wants to rule Birca?" asked Frode, his voice incredulous. "Why would he not lay claim after defeating Tarben?" He took the fur from his shoulders and Vali recognised it as his own.

"Mayhap he did not know Tarben had fallen?"

"You think he means to ransom Brenna for the jarldon?" asked Ragnar.

"I think he wants the Valkyrie of Birca out of action," replied Vali.

"So why not kill her with her husband?" said Frode.

"Only the gods know." Vali fastened his fur.

"You'll go after her?" asked Ragnar.

"I'm the only sober warrior in this town," he retorted, heading for the door.

"You love her."

Vali stopped in his tracks.

"You won't stop until she is safe."

Ragnar's acknowledgement brought a tension across his shoulders, the old resentment tasting bitter in his throat.

"I'll leave now and travel alone."

"No, I'll come with you," protested Frode.

"You'll only slow me down."

"The huscarl will be close behind you," said Ragnar.

"If you're right about Tingvalla, Sigurd will be expecting them."

"Not if I send them in the other direction."

Vali turned to face the older man. Ragnar would never defy his King!

"I don't know what Sigurd wants with Brenna." Ragnar stepped closer, almost pleading with him. "If he's taken her to Tingvalla, there is no way twenty men will prevail. Even with Odin on their side."

"If Aric finds out you've misled him-"

"I do not know where Sigurd has taken Brenna, not for sure."

"Your instincts do not usually fail you, Ragnar."

"Which is why I came to you."

They held each other's stare, one determined and the other desperate. Ragnar clasped Vali's forearm. "May the gods go with you."

30

*B*renna woke to a voice issuing instructions and a full moon that had risen fully in the sky above. She raised her hand to rub her eyes, only to find her wrists bound. Wiggling her feet confirmed her ankles were bound as well.

"Relax, Valkyrie."

A shadow fell across her face. Sigurd blocked the moon.

"You took quite a blow to the head."

He chuckled as he stepped aside and the sudden light of the moon blinded her.

Once her eyes adjusted, she glanced around her surroundings. She was lying in the bottom of what appeared to be a karvi, rather than one of the drakkar warships she'd seen Sigurd's army retreating in after the first battle at Birca. The smaller vessel carried only a small crew of a dozen men, including those that had attacked her and Ubbe. The sail was lowered and men were at the oars. They must be close to their destination.

Using her elbows, she pushed herself into a sitting position. Her head began to pound, reminding her of the manner by which she'd been captured. The barely dried blood of her slain husband stained her pale green wedding gown.

No, she couldn't allow herself to wallow. Not if she wanted to live.

She strained her neck in order to see over the bow. A silvery coastline was in view. Judging by the height of the moon, she hadn't been unconscious for long. And with land in sight, they'd travelled inland, not via the sea. This must be Tingvalla, Sigurd's captured stronghold.

Easing herself back against the side of the boat, she tentatively examined the back of her head with her fingers. A lump was already forming where the handle of Sigurd's axe had connected. Her fingertips were clear, so the skin had not been broken. Still, her head throbbed without mercy.

Closing her eyes, she tried to understand Sigurd's motive in bringing her to Tingvalla. After losing two battles, she imagined his forces must be quite depleted. Surely, he didn't think to mount a defence against Aric from here? Brenna thought back to their encounter at Birca. What had he said just before he'd put his axe through Ubbe's head?

Ubbe had asked Sigurd what he wanted. She fought the bile rising in her throat as her last memories of Ubbe returned. Regardless of what she'd thought of him as her intended husband, he did not deserve to die without a sword in hand. He did not deserve to never feast in the halls of Valhalla.

Your land. Your title... Your wife!

Her eyes sprang open.

That's what Sigurd had said. What could he be planning? Another attack? He'd just killed the Jarl of Birca, yet he had not claimed the land for himself. It made no sense. He could have taken her as his prisoner to face Aric and proclaim Birca as his. Then Sigurd would have Ubbe's land, his title... and his wife. With an understrength army, surely that would have been the most effective course of action.

"Allfather, lend me your sight so that I may understand what this brute intends," she muttered.

The stroke of the oars ceased. They were about to beach on the shore of Tingvalla. There was no need for stealth on his own land, and Sigurd shouted his orders. Half of the men disembarked, their feet splashing into the fjord, hands gripping the karvi to guide it safely onto the beach. Brenna was jolted as the boat found land. With her hands and ankles bound, she had little balance and was thrown onto her side. Her barely receding headache brought back to the fore. Rough hands dragged her upright using the ropes around her wrists.

Sigurd pulled her close, his breath hot on her face.

"It would give me great pleasure if you were to try and fight me, Valkyrie," he growled. "I enjoy it when my woman asks to be disciplined."

Brenna squared her shoulders, denying the instinct to pull away from him.

"I am not your woman."

He smirked, his teeth glinting in the moonlight. "You will be soon enough."

Sigurd ducked beneath her elbows and hoisted her over his shoulder. With two strides they were out of the karvi and making their way towards the sleeping village. Again, Brenna resisted her impulse to struggle. Sucking in a deep breath and trying to control her thundering heart, she made herself focus and take in as much of her surroundings as possible.

It seemed the dock was further up the shore. She could make out the distant shape of the drakkar warships. Movement caught her eye and she assumed the longboats were guarded as there was not enough activity to suggest naught but the night watch roaming the dock. There were no torches lit anywhere along the shoreline. An attempt to make the village appear deserted to anyone coming in search of her, mayhap?

They reached the longhouses and Brenna could smell the smoke from fires warming those that slept within. She could detect no other movement, other than Sigurd and his men returning from the fjord. They walked in silence, their footsteps echoing in the night. As they moved further into the village, a warm glow began to melt the silvery light of the moon. Judging by the shape of the buildings and structures, they were passing through the marketplace, albeit a much smaller one than Birca's.

A soft murmur underscored the men's trudging footfall. The glow became brighter. Without warning, a cheer erupted, filling the empty night with a crescendo of noise. Sigurd placed her on her feet and she found herself in the middle of a sea of Vikings. As far as her eyes could travel, she saw warriors. There were hundreds of them, surrounding her. Suffocating her with their roar.

Sigurd raised his arms and the crowd quietened.

"Behold," he bellowed. "The Valkyrie of Birca."

The din rose, then trebled in volume.

Brenna straightened her spine and raised her chin. She would not let them think she was intimidated, even though her heart clamoured inside her chest as loudly as her enemy cheered and jeered. Surely, her eyes were deceiving her. Sigurd had lost so many men in the preceding battles. Where had these warriors come from? She willed herself to stay steady.

Don't show them fear.

The swish of a sword being unsheathed brought a hush to the army once more. Sigurd walked toward her, led by his sword. Just breathe. Was this his plan, to spill her blood in front of his men as... what? Retribution? A sacrifice to the gods? Her hands and feet were bound, she had no weapon. Was his purpose to ensure her seat at Valhalla was left empty? Acid churned in her belly, while fear raced up her spine.

He brought the tip of his sword to her throat. Across the polished metal, she glared at the brute. Sigurd held her stare for a moment before dropping the sword and stepping closer. He gave her another smirk, slowly circling around her using the tip of his sword to lift the skirt of her gown.

Brenna began to shake all over. From behind, Sigurd gathered her skirt into his free hand, exposing her calves to the night air.

The fear intensified. Did he mean to humiliate her in front of his men? To rape her before he murdered her? Despite the thick rope around her hands, they began to shake. The tip of the sword traced a jagged line on her inner leg. When it reached her knees, Sigurd pushed the flat of his sword between them. Her breath caught in her throat, her mind racing with the possibilities of what may follow.

Sigurd chuckled in her ear. The noise of the crowd had faded from her consciousness. Her only thought was the sword and in which direction he might wield it.

"Freya, help me," she whispered.

The sword descended, then sawed through the rope binding her ankles. Sigurd dropped her skirts as relief washed over her, threatening to turn her legs to water. She found the strength to remain standing and forced herself to face Sigurd as he positioned himself in front of her again.

Her breath came hard and fast. He was enjoying watching her suffer.

"Raise your hands, Valkyrie."

Clenching her hands into separate fists to try and control the shaking, she did as she was ordered. He pushed the sword between her wrists and began sawing through the ropes. In seconds her hands were free. She held them in place a moment before bringing them back to her sides. Her galloping heartbeat kept time with the howling bloodlust of the men watching Sigurd toy with her.

Anger replaced her fear and humiliation. If his intent was to kill her, she prayed to the gods he gave her a sword with which to defend herself. Every muscle in her body ached to hack his head from his body and dare any of his warriors to take her on. She would not be so hesitant to claim Tingvalla and Sigurd's army as her own.

Sigurd gave a nod to the men who had accompanied him to Birca. They formed a u-shaped guard around her.

"Come," he said before turning his back on her.

The crowd parted as he walked forward, revealing a hall. Her nails bit into the palms of her hands. With no other option presenting itself, she followed Sigurd.

Inside the hall, a fire burned in the pit running up the centre of the main room. Outside, her emotions had dominated and she hadn't been aware that she was cold until the fire began to warm her. Long tables ran along either side of the fire pit, with benches pushed beneath them. Skins and furs lined the floor along the walls, forming sleeping quarters. Another table ran along the far end of the room, a large chair covered in skins sat in the centre. Curtains hung behind this table. Brenna guessed they separated Sigurd's sleeping chamber and the kitchen from the hall.

Sigurd took his seat on the chair, gesturing for Brenna to

sit beside him on the bench. His men divided, with half sitting at one of the long tables, and the others sitting on the other side of the hall. To ensure she couldn't escape, she guessed. She would stay alert and wait for an opportunity to plan her escape.

Brenna stood to the left of the fire pit. Slaves appeared with food and beer and the men wasted no time beginning their meal, including Sigurd. She continued to stand there. It was only moments ago she was standing bound outside, sure she was about to meet a terrifying end. Now, life went on around her and it seemed she was expected to adapt.

"Valkyrie," Sigurd's voice snapped her attention back to him. "Sit. Eat."

"I'm not hungry."

"Sit."

He did not raise his eyes to hers as he stuffed meat into his mouth.

Still feeling shaky on her legs, she moved around the table and sat halfway along the bench. Sigurd glanced in her direction.

"I don't bite." He jerked his head, indicating she should move closer.

Brenna did not move, the glare returning to her eye. A slave handed her a drinking horn filled with beer. She took a long draught, her thirst suddenly insatiable.

She had the distinct impression her death was not Sigurd's plan. Her anger drove her to impatience. "Why did you not claim Birca after you killed the Jarl?"

"Which Jarl?"

She breathed out in frustration. "Not Tarben. You were not even present on the battlefield."

Sigurd dropped the portion of meat in his hand and turned in his seat to look at her. "Oh, I was there, Valkyrie."

"You did not fight."

"Ja, that is true. I wanted to watch." He gestured for a slave to fill his drinking horn.

"What were you looking for?" she asked.

"I was waiting for the gods to show me how I was to become the Jarl of Birca."

Brenna frowned. "Killing the Jarl was not enough?"

"Mayhap," he shrugged. "If you hadn't outsmarted my army."

"You were defeated."

"So, you claim, Valkyrie." Sigurd returned to his food, the grease from the meat glistening on his fingers.

"Your army retreated. They ran away."

"The one on the battlefield, ja."

Anger and exasperation collided. "You were defeated."

"I chose to not send forth the other hundred warriors I had waiting behind the mountain top."

This made no sense to Brenna. The brute must be lying. "One hundred, fresh warriors would have ensured your victory."

"I saw something else I wanted."

Repulsion crawled across her skin. Sigurd looked up and burst into laughter.

"I'm sure you'll make an adequate bed mate, Valkyrie, but you are not the prize."

"Speak plainly, Sigurd. What is it you want?"

He slammed his fists down on the table, the action causing Brenna to flinch and the conversations at the other tables to stop.

"What I want is the Jarldom of Birca to be given to me."

She shook her head, not understanding.

"I was born the son of a slave, no better than one myself. I have had to fight for everything. And I am tired of it." His eyes burned with rage. "I want the King to name me as the Jarl of Birca."

"You believe King Aric will name you as Jarl?" her tone underscored her incredulity.

"Ja. And you, Valkyrie, will be my wife."

"You think by forcing me to marry you, Aric will make you Jarl?"

He laughed again, long and loud. Fury coursed through her veins. Finally, he wiped the mirth from his eyes. "I believe Aric will make me the Jarl and give me your hand in marriage once he understands the size of the army he faces."

Understanding dawned. Sigurd craved legitimacy. But what had any of this to do with her? As though he could hear her thoughts, he answered her unspoken question.

"I have heard the stories, Valkyrie. The wanderers already sing of all you have done. The people of Birca look to you for leadership. They look to you for compassion. Aric's hand may be forced by the size of my army, but the people will only accept me if you are my wife."

"You underestimate Aric and the people of Birca."

"Nei, I believe you underestimate your worth to Aric and Birca. The King will agree to my terms, you'll see." Sigurd pushed back his chair and stood. "You may as well become accustomed to me."

31

*V*ali took a small fishing boat, built for one or two men only. His oars sliced through the water, the full moon lighting his way. He could think of only one reason Sigurd would take Brenna: to force himself upon the Valkyrie of Birca. He pulled harder, urging the small craft faster through the water. The craftsmanship of the vessel was not that of a drakkar or other longboat; it hadn't been built for speed. Luckily, the night was still and the water calm, making up a little for the bulky design.

The look of desperation on Ragnar's face played on his mind. He feared for his daughter. So much so, he was prepared to risk the wrath of Aric if he learned of his betrayal. Yet, he'd also acknowledged the strength of Vali's love for Brenna. Knowing he would stop at nothing to bring her home safely.

He drew the oars up and looked over his shoulder. The dark shoreline of Tingvalla had turned silver under the moonlight. He was close. Putting the oars back into position, he pulled harder, knowing every minute counted. It felt like an eternity, but minutes later he was lugging the fishing boat onto the shore. He dragged it towards a thicket of trees, hoping it would provide enough cover to hide the vessel.

No torches lit the dock but he detected movement - a guard for Sigurd's warships, no doubt. Mayhap Ragnar had been wrong in assuming the brute would bring Brenna to Tingvalla. Although, given the heavy losses he'd sustained in the previous battles, there was a chance he did not have guards to spare. Still, Vali remained vigilant for lookouts as he crept towards the village.

It sounded as if a feast were underway. Even from the shore, Vali could hear the sound of cheering and howling. He could not hear music, which seemed strange if it was a feast or celebration of some kind. He moved fast, staying low. There was no one about the longhouses or market-place. They must all be at the feast.

Torchlight glowed from beyond the marketplace. The noise was deafening. Fear wrapped itself around his heart. Would Sigurd bring Brenna here to sacrifice her to the gods? The frenzied cacophony added weight to the notion. He swallowed hard and picked up his pace, walking through the village with purpose, as though he belonged.

Rounding the corner, Vali stopped short at the scene in front of him. Hundreds of warriors were gathered in some sort of clearing. He couldn't see what was happening over the heads and shoulders of those in front of him. His heart galloped in his chest. He needed to get to higher ground.

Skirting the gathering, he spied a structure resembling a forge. Checking to ensure the building was empty, he scaled the external walls until he reached the rooftop. Pulling himself up, he shimmied across the peak until he could see the centre of the crowd. He shifted until his body hugged the fall of the roof not exposed to the people below.

The number of warriors was astounding. But his atten-

tion was focused on the woman in the middle of it all -
Brenna. A man dressed from head to toe in black had just
cut the ropes round her wrists and gestured for her to follow
him. The crowd parted and he walked to a large structure
Vali guessed was the hall. Brenna followed, escorted by
warriors on either side.

She held her head high and walked unaided, but Vali
could sense her fear. Where was that bastard taking her?
Pushing back from the peak of the roof, he manoeuvred
himself to the ground, then headed towards the hall.
Thankfully, the warriors stayed put for the moment,
chanting and shouting. He used the noise as cover for his
footfall as he ran to the side of the hall. There were no open-
ings to see inside. Moving around the building, he found the
only other exit was from the kitchen, which was full of
slaves and servants.

Cursing, he needed to find higher ground in order to
watch who came and went from the hall. If the gods were
with him, they'd move Brenna to another location and
provide an easier solution to his current predicament.

He chose a single structure, probably the sleeping hut
for the slaves that served in Sigurd's household, behind the
hall. He climbed to the top and found a spot from which he
could watch the comings and goings from both the kitchen
entrance and enough of the main entrance for those
heading back to the longhouses.

The warriors had begun to disperse from the clearing.
As they walked away from the hall, Vali had to assume some
of them would take up watch positions along the shore,
mayhap relieving some of the guards from the dock. Surely,
Sigurd would be prepared for Aric to retaliate.

He returned his gaze to the hall. No one had come in or
out. He could hear nothing. That had to be a good thing. If

Sigurd was hurting Brenna, he would know... wouldn't he? He would hear her screams or signs of a struggle. He sent a silent prayer to Odin to keep her safe until he could rescue her.

A shadow loomed from the main entrance. One of the guards made his way towards Vali, his footsteps echoing in the night. When the Viking got near the hut, he veered to the left. He relieved himself against a tree, belching loudly as he did so. Vali peered over the edge and was thankful for the still night. A cesspit had been dug not far from where the Viking stood. The lack of breeze kept the smell contained. Vali hoped it remained so.

The Viking returned to the hall. The more time passed, the more anxious Vali grew. What was happening inside? His imagination began to run wild again. He forced himself to focus on the hall. If many of the Vikings slept in that building, he would need to wait until they retired for the evening. Once the slaves made their way to the sleeping hut, he could find a way inside the hall, locate Brenna and free her.

Movement at the front of the hall interrupted his planning. Brenna appeared, gripped at either arm by two of Sigurd's men.

"Mayhap a night in the cold will warm your heart to me, Valkyrie." Sigurd's voice boomed from inside.

Vali watched as Brenna was escorted to one of the structures behind the forge. From his brief glance at it earlier, it appeared to be a holding pen for animals. He lost sight of Brenna and the guards, however, more of Sigurd's men came out of the hall and headed towards the cesspit. Vali crouched low against the roof of the slave hut, waiting for an opportunity to move. Eventually, the men made their way back inside. Moments later, the slaves exited the back entrance, heading for the hut he was perched upon. No guard accompanied them so they were not locked inside.

He wanted to get off the roof while there was still movement inside the hut and any noise he made might be covered by the slaves. Suddenly, another shaft of light shone through the night. A figure emerged through a hidden doorway. There was no handle on the outside, and the man pushed the door against the wall to keep it open. He was dressed in black, similar to the man who had cut Brenna's ropes earlier. Vali squinted, trying to get a better look at his face. This must be Sigurd. Regardless, he was determined to slit this man's throat.

Edging back until his feet dangled from the roof, Vali looked at the drop beneath him. It wasn't too far to jump, but it would alert the man to his presence. He didn't look as though he carried a weapon, but he would still have time to call for help. Vali waited until he heard the door close behind the man he was almost positive was Sigurd the Black.

He dropped to the ground and waited to see if anyone noticed. When no-one stirred, he crept around the hut towards the holding pen. One guard stood outside the door. He'd not noticed the other return to the hall. Quickly, he scouted the area but saw no sign of the other Viking, or anyone else. He withdrew his dagger and closed the gap between him and the guard, opening the man's throat before he could react. Vali dragged the body behind the holding pen.

Grunting from inside the enclosure sounded. Brenna! He had to get to her; save her from whatever the other guard was inflicting upon her. Bursting through the door, he found the second Viking on top of her. He was lying face forward, his eyes bulging as the rope around his neck prevented air from getting to his lungs.

Pushing his lifeless body from on top of her, Brenna moved onto her knees and searched the body, pulling a dagger from his belt. Panting for breath, she cut herself free.

"Vali?"

Her surprise was fleeting. "Did you kill the other guard?"

"Ja..." said Vali. "Are you hurt?"

"Nei. How many are with you?"

"I am alone."

Standing, she looked him in the eye. "Alone? Why are you here?"

"To rescue you."

Brenna held his gaze, then looked at the dead Viking at her feet.

"I see."

32

"*I* have a boat hidden near the shore," said Vali, standing inside the door of the hut.

Brenna knelt over the dead Viking. "Nei, Sigurd has sent forty men to watch for Aric. We would not get past them."

"Over land?"

Brenna looked up at him; her would-be rescuer. Vali's presence complicated her plan. Yet her heart warmed that he had come for her.

"Ja, although I think we should find someplace to rest."

"I thought you were not hurt?" His face twisted with concern.

"I am well, but I am tired, Vali. An hour to rest is all I need. No one will know I am gone until the sun rises."

She held her breath as Vali regarded her. It was not like her to require respite in the height of battle.

Finally, he nodded. "We will rest, but only once we are well away from Tingvalla."

"Thank you."

She set to removing the dead Viking's belt. She cut a

third from the leather strap and fashioned it into a belt around her calf, securing the dagger in place.

"Let's go."

Vali peered around the door. Once satisfied they would not be detected, he motioned for her to follow him. Dragging the fur from the guard to wrap around her shoulders, she kept close to Vali. She'd not seen him at the wedding, nor the feast. Yet he was here. But what of her parents? Where was Ragnar?

They crept between buildings, heading for a dense cluster of trees to hide them from the light of the full moon. The terrain became steeper as they climbed above the village. Unlike Birca, there was no farming land. Mountains and rock, trees and foliage were all that hugged Tingvalla. There didn't appear to be any scouts in this area. Mayhap, higher up. They moved cautiously, nonetheless.

Reaching the peak of the mountain, they found shelter within a small cave. From their vantage point, they could see the village and the fjord. If Aric sent his men, they would know. Despite the night chill, they dared not light a fire, instead huddling close together to share body heat.

"How did you get here, Vali?" she whispered once she was settled in his arms.

"Ragnar sent me."

"My father? What of Aric's men?"

Vali explained Ragnar's motivation, and how he came to be the only sober warrior in Birca.

"It was a good plan," agreed Brenna, warming a little on the inside to hear Ragnar chose her over duty to the King. "Attacking Tingvalla would have been walking into a trap."

"Sigurd's army, it is much larger than anyone could anticipate." Vali shifted against the cave wall.

Brenna repeated what Sigurd had told her of his plan to be made the Jarl of Birca by the King.

"Why does he want you for his wife?"

She sighed. "Sigurd believes the people will accept him if I am by his side."

She felt Vali stiffen and his arms squeezed a little tighter around her. "But if the King proclaims him Jarl, the people will have no choice but to accept him."

"Mayhap..." her voice drifted away as she contemplated her exchange with Sigurd.

"What is it?" asked Vali.

"Sigurd could have claimed me as his bride tonight, or at least forced himself upon me as master. Yet he did not."

Vali stroked her hair, allowing her to order her thoughts.

"He wants me by his side willingly."

"Everything I've heard of Sigurd suggests he is a tyrant who takes what he wants, at any cost."

Brenna nodded, Vali's tender ministrations were soothing the ache that still throbbed in her skull. "He spoke of being the son of a slave, less than naught. I believe he is seeking acknowledgement."

"Of what?"

She shook her head.

"Who sired him?"

"He did not say."

"Mayhap he has the notion that his father is someone of importance?" suggested Vali.

Brenna thought of her own ambitions and her longheld belief that her mother was robbed of her rightful place as Queen of Gyldarhagi. Hertha may have made her peace with never sitting on the throne, but Brenna still wanted to rule. It was in her blood. Could Sigurd be the same?

"It's a possibility," she agreed.

"Rest now, we have a long walk back to Birca. Unless you prefer to find a new home?"

She turned to face him. "A new home?"

Vali's eyes lit up. "We could go somewhere else, far away. We could be together."

"And leave Birca and the King unprepared for Sigurd and his army? Nei, we cannot."

He took her face in his hands and placed his lips on her forehead. "Brenna, I love you. Only you. I cannot watch you return to Birca and marry another to satisfy the King."

Anger sparked deep within her. "You think Aric would agree to Sigurd's plan?"

Vali shrugged. "Who knows? If not Sigurd, then another. You are the Valkyrie of Birca."

"An asset to be bartered," she muttered.

Vali remained silent.

Would she never have the right to choose her own path? Returning to Birca would mean returning to the will of Aric. He was her King. Yet Ragnar had sent Vali to rescue her, could she rely on her father to speak for her?

It mattered naught. In her heart, she knew she could not run away with Vali and leave Birca to face Sigurd and his army without warning.

Of course, Sigurd may insist she was part of the deal and she would be hunted and brought back to Birca. He would kill Vali for sure. Mayhap claim he kidnapped her... kept her from her rightful place at his side.

Nei, she must go through with the plan she came up with as she listened to Sigurd reveal her fate. She must end this threat and then face Aric and her father and make them hear her. Make them understand. She would no longer be a pawn in matters of territory and rule.

"What are you thinking?" Vali's gentle voice interrupted her thoughts.

"I cannot run away, Vali."

She felt his frustration rise. "You are not the Jarl of Birca. You are a prize for the Jarl of Birca. That is what you will remain if we return."

"And what am I if I run away with you?" she challenged.

"You would be my wife and I will keep you safe from men like Sigurd and Aric who would use you for their own advantage."

"You would keep me safe?" Brenna shuffled out of his arms. "I do not need you to keep me safe."

"Marrying me will release you from the will of Aric."

"And what of my will?"

They stared at each other in the darkness of the cave.

"You do not wish to marry me?" His voice was soft.

She moved closer to take his hands in hers. "Vali, I love you. It is you I want to be with. But I cannot marry you simply to avoid being bartered to another by the King."

He squeezed her hands in his. "Marry me because you want to."

Her heart clenched. Marriage was not something she could contemplate. Not when the sun had only just set on her wedding to Ubbe. Not when men saw marriage to her as the solution to a problem.

"I love you, Vali. Let that be enough for now."

A shadow of hurt passed across his eyes. Brenna clutched his hands, willing him to understand. Willing him to let the subject drop for now.

"Come, let us rest a while. I need to close my eyes," she said.

Vali nodded and she shifted back into his arms. She

knew she'd caused him pain, but she would not be dissuaded from her plan. The moon had begun its descent and there were only a few hours before the sun would rise. She didn't have much time.

33

*B*renna waited until Vali's breathing fell into a slow and steady rhythm before slipping out of his arms. She left the dead Viking's fur across his body in the hope that Vali wouldn't miss her weight and warmth against him until she'd completed her task.

From the mouth of the cave, she scanned the fjord. She saw no longboats on the horizon. Below, Tingvalla appeared to sleep. The misdirection Ragnar had given Aric's men had bought her time, but that time was running out. She expected a drakkar full of warriors would be on their way to take their revenge on Sigurd soon.

Her progress was faster coming down the mountain, using the trees and foliage to hide her movements. Once she reached the slave hut she waited, watching the mountain from which she'd come for any signs of disturbance. If Vali had woken, he would come after her. If Sigurd had scouts along the ridge line, she prayed they had not noticed her descent. When all remained still, she continued to the hall.

Vali had mentioned the hidden door when he'd asked her about Sigurd. She removed the dagger from the strap around her calf. Running her hands across the timber, she located the narrow slit between the wall and the door. She wedged the dagger between the two, slowly prying the door open. Thank the gods, Sigurd had not bolted the door from the inside.

A fire burned low in the pit beside the bed, illuminating the room with a soft glow. Soundlessly, she moved forward. Sigurd lay sprawled across the bed, a fur covering little of his naked body. Even in his sleep, the brute looked no less evil. Brenna could not look at him without remembering the sickening crack of the axe splitting Ubbe's head. Or the way he'd toyed with her, placing his sword between her legs while she imagined all manner of horrors.

She swallowed the rising revulsion and fear. Clenching her fists, she brought her breathing under control.

"Are you just going to stand there all night, Valkyrie?"

The deep rumble of his voice forced her nails to dig deeper into the flesh of her palm. She slipped the dagger back into the belt on her leg.

"Tell me, was it the cold or me that brought you inside?"

"One of your warriors offered to keep the chill from my bones," she replied, stepping closer to the bed.

"And did you allow him?"

"Nei."

"And did you do him the courtesy of killing him with a weapon in his hand?"

"His weapons were at hand; he chose not to use them."

Sigurd's chuckle echoed off the walls and ceiling. "He was instructed not to lay hands on you. You were right to kill him."

Brenna bowed her head, acknowledging his dismissal of her actions.

"Why are you here, Valkyrie? If it is to kill me, you don't

appear to be carrying a weapon. While I don't doubt your prowess on the battlefield, you could not defeat me in my own bed."

She stepped closer still, holding her hands before her. "I have no sword, as you can see."

Sigurd sat up, allowing the fur to fall from him completely, revealing his hardening cock. He began to stroke himself, waiting for her to continue.

"It seems you and I are not so dissimilar, Sigurd."

"How so, Valkyrie?"

"We both want power; to rule." Her heart beat steadily in her chest as she came to stand beside the bed. Her hand did not shake as she traced one finger along his chest. "For others to acknowledge our abilities and reward us as we are due."

Sigurd smiled up at her. Her stomach turned yet she maintained her composure. He grasped her wrists and pulled her closer.

"What is it you want right now, Valkyrie?"

She smiled, his breath tickling her lips. "It is still my wedding night, is it not?"

His lips covered hers and she willed herself not to pull away. Wrapping her free hand around his shoulders, she kneeled on the bed, straddling him as his tongue began to probe her mouth. She responded with her own tongue, tangling her fingers in his dark hair. Releasing her wrist, his hands found her backside. She let a low moan escape.

He lifted her hips, trying to find her entrance with his cock. Pushing him down against the bed, she held his gaze. Her fingers unfastened the ties at each of her shoulders, allowing her gown to fall to her hips. Sigurd devoured her breasts with hooded eyes. She offered him a small smile and started to rock her hips, rubbing along his shaft.

His grin was menacing in the candle light, the scar along his face more pronounced. He reached for her breasts, taking one in each hand. Massaging and pinching her nipples. She kept rocking against him, deepening her breathing as he watched his hands work her breasts.

Reaching back to her calf, she slipped the dagger from the belt. Leaning down, her eyes on his mouth, she used her tongue to wet her own lips.

"I want you, Valkyrie."

She moved forward as he grabbed his cock around the base and pulled it into position for her to ease herself back onto. She leaned closer, one hand entwining into his hair. She pulled his locks harder, holding him in place.

He grinned. "You like to be in charge, Valkyrie?"

"Always," she whispered.

"I think I can allow it. For one night."

"Then I better make the most of it."

She drew the blade up and across his throat, using all of her strength to cut through. He had one hand on his cock and the other on her breast, both trapped beneath her body. His eyes bulged and his mouth gaped.

"Birca, the jarldom and I, will never belong to you."

She kept her grip on his hair and sawed at his neck until the light faded from his eyes. Power thrummed through her veins. Sitting upright, she pulled her gown into place and tightened the fastenings. She wiped the dagger clean in an X-shape across her chest, covering Ubbe's dried blood with that of his murderers.

"A Valkyrie has the right to choose who is worthy to join Odin and his Einharjar. Sigurd, you are not worthy. May Ubbe find his way to the Allfather."

She dipped two fingers into Sigurd's blood that had spilled down his chest. Running her fingers from her forehead, across her eyelids and down her cheeks, she whispered, "I offer this sacrifice to you, Freya, to right the wrongs of this day and to pray for more peaceful and prosperous days to come."

Rising from the bed, she smoothed her skirt into place. Across the room stood Sigurd's fur and weapons. With a last glance at the slain brute, she crossed the room and wrapped his fur across her shoulders. Tightening his belt around her waist, she slid the sword and axe at either side, careful to fix them so they would not trail along the ground. Finally, she picked up the black shield interlaid with a golden eagle, and the spear.

Sigurd had gathered this army of warriors with a promise of riches and land. They did not follow him out of a sense of loyalty, of that she was certain. With their leader dead, Brenna would offer them a choice to leave without consequence, or join her people at Birca or the King at Fornsigtuna. She had no idea if this would work, and prayed to the gods that Aric was on his way with reinforcements.

She took a steadying breath and entered the hall. Brenna stepped up onto the bench, and then onto the central table; she surveyed the sleeping warriors. Most had been with Sigurd in Birca and on the longboat. These were his most trusted warriors. Yet he had died only a short distance from where they slept, at the hand of a woman they had witnessed taken and locked away outside. It was time they met the Valkyrie.

She raised Sigurd's spear and threw it into the centre of the room. The spear reverberated as it hit the floor, once, twice.

The Vikings stirred.

"What is it, Sigurd?"

"Has Aric finally found his way across the water?"

"Sigurd is dead."

All heads snapped to attention in the direction of Brenna's voice. Some jumped to their feet. Others simply stared. Some of the slaves crept from the kitchen into the hall.

"He is your master no longer."

"You killed him?" asked one Viking.

"Ja, and offered his blood to Freya."

The silence weighed heavily. Brenna let her stare move to each man, looking them each in the eye for any sign of challenge or dissent.

"You truly are Valkyrie."

Others mumbled in assent.

"I am guided by the gods, that much is true. I will not answer to any man."

The mumbling grew in volume as the men looked to each other for direction.

Brenna's voice carried over the top of them. "You need not fear your own fate. I have a plan that will serve each of you well."

Laying out her proposition, she instructed the Vikings to spread the word and have each man and woman make their choice by day's end.

Brenna remained on the table as she gave her orders. "Relieve the scouts on the dock. I wish to be informed the moment Aric's longboats are spied. No one is to engage them in combat."

"What of Tingvalla, lady?"

"Tingvalla does not belong to you. King Aric may determine the future of this place."

The Vikings dispersed. Brenna sent the slaves to prepare the morning meal and stoke the fires. Climbing down from the table, she walked towards the main doors. The first rays of sunlight glowed on the horizon. She stepped out to meet the new day.

———

34

*T*he drop in temperature caused Vali to stir, it was always coldest before the sun rose. They had slept much longer than they'd intended. He reached for Brenna and found only empty space. He sat up straighter, fully alert.

"Brenna?" he hissed.

She was not in the cave. Mayhap she had gone to relieve herself. He crawled to the mouth of the cave and peered into the darkness. The moon no longer sat high enough in the sky to light up the night.

"Brenna?"

Nothing.

He listened to the night, hoping to get a sense of where she had gone. When she did not return after a few minutes, he realised she had indeed left him in the cave. But to do what? Return to Birca without him? Or face Sigurd? It was possible she'd been spotted by one of his scouts and taken prisoner again. With more questions forming and no answers presenting themselves, Vali decided he must return to Tingvalla. If Brenna was there, she would be in danger.

Wrapping the fur around himself, he gathered his weapons. Another inspection of the landscape revealed no movement, so he set out for the village. His heart thumped against his chest as surely as Thor himself was trapped inside and he found it hard to catch his breath. Why would she leave without telling him? If she'd been captured, she wouldn't return willingly after only just escaping Sigurd's clutches.

Vali's foot slipped on uneven ground. Cursing, he made himself focus on getting down the mountain in one piece and undetected. He was no good to Brenna injured. He slowed his pace, listening for any sign he was being pursued. Peering through the foliage, he searched the dark waters of the fjord. It made sense for Aric to wait until now if he was going to face Sigurd on his own land; the full moon would have cast too much light and their presence would have been detected well before they reached the shore. Aric couldn't know that forty Vikings awaited him.

Movement caught his eye. He strained to make sense of the dark shadows behind the hall. Dull light glowed from the far side of the hall - the kitchen? It must be the slaves beginning their day before the sun rose. He didn't have long if he wanted to get into the village before the Vikings woke en masse.

He wondered again if Brenna had left by herself to try and warn the King. But why not take him with her? He shook the conflicting thoughts from his mind and began his descent once more. It seemed more likely Brenna had returned to Tingvalla, either willingly or by force if she had been found outside the cave.

Two muffled cracks echoed in the night. Vali crouched low, holding his breath and scanning the sleeping village for the source of the sound. He saw naught.

Wait, was the noise coming from the hall? The slaves were inside. Mayhap they'd displeased their master. He picked up the pace, breaking into a run until he reached the hall and pressed himself against the wall. His breath was ragged and heavy, fear prickling his spine. He knew he was going into this blind, but he had no time. The sun, and the village, was about to rise. He must find Brenna.

A creaking whoosh, followed by a thud to his left brought his hand to the hilt of his sword. Voices muttered, footsteps... more than one man. They were exiting the hall. Vali edged closer, keeping his back to the wall, until he reached the corner. About twenty Vikings were heading in different directions - to the longhouses, the docks. Fists pounded against the sides and doors of the longhouses. Whatever was going on, it was about to commence.

Would Brenna be locked back in the animal pens? He tried to think positively, mayhap she was hiding there, waiting for... what? Odin, help him, where was she? He released his hold on his sword and removed his axe. He would check the outbuildings around the marketplace and hope he was quick enough to avoid Sigurd's men. He tightened his hold on his axe and checked his surroundings.

Clear.

He started for the first building.

"Vali!"

Was he dreaming?

He pivoted, half expecting to find Brenna in Sigurd's clutches.

He was dreaming.

Brenna stood at the entrance of the halls, both doors open wide behind her. She wore a long black fur and weapons sheathed against her body. Blood stained her face, painted in the manner of war and ritual. She held a black and gold shield on one arm, and a spear in the other. She was no one's prisoner.

"Brenna," he moved towards her. "What is this?"

"Freedom," she replied.

"What do you mean?" The axe fell to his side.

"I have freed Birca from the threat of Sigurd."

"How?" His eyes travelled up and down her body, still not comprehending what he was looking upon.

"Sigurd is dead."

Vali felt as though he was seeing Brenna for the first time. He knew her as beautiful and brave. He knew her as fierce and a fighter. He knew her as caring and compassionate. But he had never seen her for who she truly was. He'd been so blinded by his resentment of her ambition, he had never seen all of her qualities combined. She appeared before him now, an amalgamation of everything he knew her to be and more. She was more than Valkyrie. She was no one's possession.

She was a true leader.

A Viking Queen.

"Lady," a voice interrupted them. Two of Sigurd's men came from behind him. "Aric's longboats have been seen along the western coast."

"What of the men waiting for them?"

"We have delivered your message, Lady. They choose to join you in Birca, as do we."

Brenna bowed her head. "You are welcome."

She turned to Vali. "I have given Sigurd's men a choice. They may leave Tingvalla without consequence, or join me at Birca or the King at Fornsigtuna."

He nodded slowly.

"I need you to return to the docks with these men. Aric must not attack, Vali. You must explain he is in no danger here."

"Ja." His feet remained rooted to the ground.

Brenna stared at him. "Vali!"

He shook his head, trying to break the spell he had fallen under. "Ja, I will bring Aric and Ragnar to you."

The Vikings beside him waited for him to move off, following behind. As he made his way to the docks, men were appearing from the longhouses. They were headed to the hall, to Brenna. He detected no hint of animosity. None of these men had been loyal to Sigurd beyond whatever he had promised or paid them. They were not kin or clan.

At the docks, the men parted to let Vali pass. A few turned to the Vikings behind him to question his presence, receiving assurances he was sent by the Valkyrie. Satisfied, they allowed him through.

Standing in front of these men, who only moments ago had formed one of the biggest armies Vali had ever seen, felt surreal. He prayed Loki had not manipulated his mind while he lay sleeping.

Two drakkars drew closer. He could see the King and Ragnar clearly at the bow of the lead ship.

"Drop your swords and shields if you do not wish to be attacked," he called to the men behind him.

Wood and metal clanked as it fell to the ground.

"Sigurd is defeated," shouted Vali. "These men have no quarrel with you, Aric."

Vali watched Ragnar and the King confer. Heard the order for the archers to lower their bows.

The longboats glided into the shore. Men disembarked, water splashing, hands guiding the ships further onto the beach. King Aric and Ragnar stepped onto the side and off, heading straight for Vali. Ragnar spoke first.

"Where is Brenna?"

"She is well," he smiled at the older man, hoping to relieve his fear.

"You defeated Sigurd?" asked Aric, distrust in his eyes.

"Nei, Sire." He raised his voice so all the men would hear his words. "The Valkyrie of Birca ended the reign of Sigurd on this land. She waits for you in the hall."

"Brenna?" whispered Ragnar.

"Ja, Brenna ended this war."

Behind the King, his men stood tall, murmuring amongst themselves of the feats of their Valkyrie, real and imagined. From behind Vali, silence.

"Are these men your prisoners?" Aric gestured to the unarmed men.

"Nei, Brenna has given them their freedom and a choice to join her at Birca, or yourself at Fornsigtuna."

The King frowned. "She does not claim Tingvalla for herself?"

"Nei."

Aric regarded Vali for a moment before speaking again. "Lead us to the hall."

Vali nodded, swivelling to face the silent Vikings, who stood aside for Vali and Aric. Vali's heart thundered in his chest; King Aric was not an easy man to read and he was not known for accepting the feats of others when he wanted the glory for himself. He had no idea how he would greet Brenna. Or even if his own misdemeanours from the previous day would be forgotten. Regardless, Vali felt sure Brenna was done bending to the will of men. Whether he be a Viking King, or merely a Viking.

35

"*L*ady, the King approaches."

Brenna nodded her thanks to Ivar, until this morning a trusted leader in Sigurd's army. The men still looked to him for leadership and Brenna was grateful for his effective style of communicating, and his willingness to follow her as his new commander. She stood in front of the central table. A number of Sigurd's warriors had taken their place at the long table on her left. The right hand table had been left for the King's men. Servants waited for her signal to bring the food.

King Aric strode into the hall, Vali and her father close behind, followed by the huscarl and some of Birca's loyal warriors. She lifted her chin and squared her shoulders. The shield and spear lay at her feet, her other weapons sheathed. Sigurd's fur still rested on her shoulders, his blood dried across her face. A sense of calm washed over her, her heart beating at its normal pace.

"King Aric." She bowed her head as the King stopped before her.

"Well met, Brenna." He waited for her to meet his gaze.

"We had come to secure your freedom from Sigurd, but I see you have already attended to that."

"You are well, Daughter?" asked Ragnar, his eyes looking her up and down as if needing further proof she was unharmed.

"Ja, Father. I am well."

Ragnar nodded, a mix of relief and pride shining in his eyes.

"I am eager to hear how you brought down Sigurd the Black and stand in his place," said the King.

"Of course," replied Brenna. "Will you take some refreshment while we speak?"

The King gestured for his men to sit at the table provided for them. He made his way behind the table. Brenna followed, aware of Vali, her father and Ivar close behind. She swallowed her gasp of surprise as the King took a seat on the bench beside the skin-covered chair. Ragnar sat beside Aric, leaving Vali and Ivar on her right. Still, she could not bring herself to sit on the chair reserved for the one of highest rank.

"Will you sit, Valkyrie?" said the King, the corner of his mouth twitching. The room seemed to hold its breath.

Regathering herself, Brenna took her place on the chair and nodded to the slaves to bring the food. The Vikings took their seats around the hall and began talking amongst themselves. Plates of bread, cheese and cold meats began to circulate.

"Start from the beginning, Brenna." The King turned on the bench to face her.

She explained how the small raiding party came out of the shadows and dispatched their escorts within seconds. How Sigurd told Ubbe he wanted his land, his title and his wife before bringing the axe upon his head. How she woke aboard the brute's karvi as they arrived in Tingvalla.

"His plan was to marry you and claim the Jarldom of Birca as his own?" Aric asked.

"Nei, he wanted you to bestow the title upon him."

She watched as the King took a piece of cheese, examined it, then replaced it on his trencher. He took a swig of water.

"And why did Sigurd believe I would do such a thing?"

"He planned to confront you with his army - of which only two thirds remain. He intended to show you what awaited you if you did not bestow the jarldom on him."

"And what of you, Valkyrie."

Brenna straightened her spine and looked Aric in the eye. "Sigurd wanted you to give me to him, as his wife."

Aric pushed his trencher away. "The Valkyrie of Birca married off to the new Jarl of Birca, all with the King's blessing."

Vali snorted. "Wouldn't be the first time."

Aric stiffened while Ragnar's shoulder slumped. Ivar continued on with his meal. Brenna maintained eye contact with the King, silently applauding Vali.

"I suppose you want me to endorse Brenna as your wife, Vali?" Aric's voice had an edge to it.

"Nei, Sire, " Vali chuckled. "I would not risk the wrath of the Valkyrie by presuming such a union on her behalf."

Silence bounced off the walls. Ragnar stopped eating, his head bowed. A sadness seemed to come over him; could it be he understood the cost of his own role in marrying Brenna off at the King's request?. Her heart ached just a little for her father.

"King Aric," Brenna's voice was gentle but firm. "I know my worth, and it is not to be bartered with. Not again."

Tension cloyed around them, holding everyone in place, barely breathing as they waited for the King's reaction. Brenna did not waver. Her earlier sense of calm had remained, guiding her and giving her the strength to face Aric on her own terms. She knew she had the support of the people, and a new army of her own. Although, she prayed to the gods she would not need to go down that path.

"And I suppose Sigurd just told you his grand plan." Aric changed the subject without acknowledging Brenna's declaration.

She dug her nails into her palms and sent another silent plea to the gods. "He did."

Aric sniffed. "Over beer and meat?"

"Ja."

Vali laughed out loud beside her and she resisted the urge to join him.

"Sigurd made his position as master plain to me upon arrival. When it became clear his intention was not to kill me, I asked him what he was planning."

A stillness came over Ragnar. She leaned forward. "Nei, Father. He did not violate me."

Ragnar closed his eyes and nodded.

"But you were his prisoner?" asked the King.

Brenna nodded.

"Why would he tell you anything of his plan?"

"I believe Sigurd wanted me to agree to his plan."

"To be his wife?"

"Ja. Just as he wanted you to make him the Jarl, rather than simply take it."

The King rapped his knuckles on the table as he contemplated this information.

"Then what happened?" asked Aric.

"Sigurd sent me to sleep in an animal pen. I killed one of

the guards just as Vali arrived to... rescue me." This time she did allow herself a tiny smirk.

"I did manage to kill the other guard first," chimed in Vali, clearly enjoying this exchange.

"Indeed," said the King.

"Vali and I took shelter in the mountains. Once Vali was asleep, I returned to the village and found my way into Sigurd's sleeping chamber."

"You killed him in his sleep?" asked Aric.

"Nei, Sigurd knew I was there. I convinced him I had changed my mind about being his wife, then slit his throat."

Ivar laughed out loud.

"King Aric, this is Ivar of Bulandshofoi." Brenna turned and nodded at Ivar.

"Ivar, you don't appear to have a lot of regret for your fallen commander."

"Nei, King Aric," said Ivar. "Sigurd the Black gathered wanderers and mercenaries to his cause. He can no longer deliver on his promises." Ivar shrugged. "We are not bound to him or seek vengeance on his behalf."

"Ja, I have heard the Valkyrie has offered these men alternatives without censure, despite their role in the previous two attacks on Birca."

Her heart beat so fast she was afraid it would burst out of her chest. Surely, he would not reverse her promises. "King Aric, one of those alternatives was to join me in Birca. They cannot replace the men we lost, but they can replenish the ranks of our fallen warriors."

Aric returned his stare to Brenna, taking her measure. "You wish to return to Birca?"

"Ja, it is my home now," she said.

"Ivar," said Aric. "How many men have chosen to follow the Valkyrie?"

"Over one hundred men, including myself."

"And the rest?"

"Half wish to accompany you to Fornsigtuna and half have already left Tingvalla. Berserkers mainly, looking for their next fight."

"What of Tingvalla?" asked Ragnar.

"I have made it clear that the future of Tingvalla is for the King to decide," said Brenna.

"You will vouch for these men, Ivar?" asked the King.

"Nei, I will vouch for myself only," said Ivar. "But I have witnessed them give their fealty to a cause. I believe they will make good on their choices."

Aric nodded.

Brenna had moved back in her chair, facing the room. She felt more of an affinity with these strangers and the warriors of Birca before her than those at her own table. Could she stay in Tingvalla if the King cast her out? Find a new home with her own people, mayhap?

The King rose from the bench and called for the attention of those in the hall.

"You will join me, Valkyrie."

He gestured for Brenna to follow him to stand in front of the table.

"Open the doors," Aric commanded.

The doors to the hall were opened. More than one hundred men were gathered in the clearing outside. Brenna felt a similar apprehension to when Sigurd had paraded her before his men. She knew naught of Aric's mind, and there was every chance he would reduce her status to widow and insist she return to Fornisgtuna. Did she have the courage to call on her warriors to defy the King?

"Come closer," called the King. "I wish to address you all."

Tables and benches were against the wall. Bodies pressed closer, taking up all the space. Still, many remained outside.

"Sigurd the Black is dead," began Aric. "The Valkyrie of Birca, snatched from her home by this vile creature, has killed him in his bed."

Brenna stood very still, waiting for Aric to reveal his intention.

"Some might say, she took her revenge and the gods smile down on her."

The men before her listened intently.

"Despite the man having no weapon."

"Naught could save him from the Valkyrie of Birca," came a voice from the back. The crowd grunted their agreement.

A shiver ran up Brenna's spine.

"Ja, it seems the Valkyrie's reputation preceded her. She is a fine and fierce shieldmaiden," said the King.

Heads nodded.

"Brenna has ended the war between us and I welcome any man who wishes to join me, either in Fornsigtuna, or Birca."

"I will follow the Valkyrie to Birca," called another voice in the crowd.

"Ja," many added their voice to his. "We will follow the Valkyrie."

A warmth spread through Brenna. Never before had she been conceived as a leader by others. A warrior and leader in battle, ja. But never as a leader in her own right.

Aric raised his hands for silence.

"Brenna, the Valkyrie of Birca, has proven her qualities as a leader stretch beyond the battlefield. The people of

Birca love her." He paused, glancing around the hall. "It seems you will follow her."

More nod and murmurs of agreement. Brenna tried hard to keep the hope that had ignited in her belly at bay.

"And that is why, from this day forward, she will be the Jarl of Birca."

A roar sounded in Brenna's head, more deafening than the cheers from the men gathered. Aric ushered her forward. Somehow, she made her feet move - one step, then another. She looked out at the sea of faces, her heart thudding against her ribs. Was she dreaming?

"All hail the Valkyrie of Birca, Jarl Brenna of Birca," shouted Ivar.

Men dropped to their knees, even those outside the hall. She looked behind her. Vali, Ivar and her father had taken a knee. Aric nodded and smiled.

She was the Jarl of Birca.

36

*T*hey returned to Birca later that day, where Aric proclaimed the threat of Sigurd the Black was no more, thanks to the Valkyrie of Birca - the new Jarl of Birca. The people celebrated with tears of joy. The following day, the King performed the ritual to bless Brenna as the Jarl. A cow was sacrificed to the gods and the town feasted once more.

Vali watched from the sidelines. Reunited with Frode and his men, they toasted the new Jarl with more enthusiasm than previously.

"So Styrimaðr, when do we sail?" asked Frode, clutching his recently refilled horn of beer.

"You wish to return to Fornsigtuna?"

"Ja, I have decided to make Nissa my wife. But that is a little difficult when I am here in Birca."

Vali clapped his friend on the shoulder. "Congratulations, may the gods bless you with many sons."

"And mayhap a daughter or two, as well," laughed Frode.

"Skal!" They drank to the health of Frode's unborn children.

"I am pleased for you. I will speak with the King and let him know we sail on the morning tide."

"I'll tell the men and ready the boat," replied Frode, his grin splitting his face.

Vali drained the last of his beer and went in search of the King. He'd not crossed paths with Aric since returning from Tingvalla. He thanked the gods he'd not told anyone of his suspicions of Aric and hoped their altercation after the wedding had been put aside.

"Vali!" Ragnar called to him from where he stood amongst the huscarl. "I was hoping to speak with you." He hurried towards him.

Brenna's father was another who he'd managed to avoid since returning to Birca. Vali had witnessed a different man to the one he knew - a vulnerable man with much to lose. Which version of Ragnar stood before him now?

"Well met, Ragnar. The gods have truly blessed this day."

"Ja, the gods smile upon Birca and the new Jarl."

The two men smiled at each other. How strange to think Brenna had achieved her ambition despite the posturing of both of them about what would best serve her interests.

Nei, not Brenna's interests, their own.

"Vali, I asked you to bring my daughter home to me. I am in your debt."

He shook his head. "Nei, Ragnar. There is no debt. Brenna did not need my aid."

A wistful smile tugged at the older man's mouth. "It seems we both underestimated our Valkyrie."

"The gods never did."

Ragnar nodded. "Regardless, I asked for your help and you gave it readily. You could have told the King of my actions, but you have not."

"In your place, I would have done the same." He offered

his arm and Ragnar clasped his forearm as Vali reciprocated. "I was on my way to see the King. I wish to sail on the morning tide to Fornsigtuna."

The men began to walk through the crowd, in the direction of the great hall where they would find Aric.

"You'll spend some time with your family?"

"Ja, and Frode is to marry."

"And when will you take to the sea again?"

Vali sighed. Without warning, his need to raid on foreign lands had left him. Mayhap it was the growing threat of war at home; or witnessing the toll of battle on families. Or the understanding that Brenna's ambitions were not purely selfish.

"I have lost my appetite for raiding."

Ragnar frowned. "What will you do?"

Now he had spoken the words out loud, Vali felt as if he'd been cut adrift. He knew his heart was not in leading his men on another raid. Yet he felt no call to do anything else. With winter approaching in a matter of weeks, he would have plenty of time to consider his options.

"Mayhap I'll help my brother-in-law on his farm. Spend some time with my mother."

Ragnar's smile was tinged with sadness. "What of Brenna?"

A dull ache flared in his chest. "It seems you were right all along, Ragnar. There is nothing I can offer Brenna. She has achieved everything she wants and needs."

"Do not be so sure of that, my friend."

"Ragnar, Vali! Come and toast our Jarl."

They had reached the great hall and King Aric stood amongst a crowd of men on the dais. Vali spied Brenna seated with her mother. She turned and smiled at him and his heart skipped a beat. Her hair was intricately braided, showcasing her high cheekbones and blue eyes. She wore a gown the colour of the deepest ocean, a circlet of gold upon her head. She radiated beauty, and power; she was every inch the handmaiden of the gods.

A drinking horn of beer was thrust into his hand. He raised the horn in tribute to Jarl Brenna, the Valkyrie of Birca, along with her father and the King. She inclined her head in acknowledgement.

"Vali, what of your plans?" asked the King.

"I wish to return to Fornsigtuna. With your permission, we will sail on the morning tide."

"Of course, of course. I thank you for your service."

He nodded his thanks. Aric's attention was wanted elsewhere and Vali found himself standing alone in the crowded hall. His gaze drifted back to Brenna, who sat silently, watching him. She glanced behind her, in the direction of her private quarters, then back to him. Raising her head to meet her there. He bowed in response, disposing of his drinking horn.

The curtain separating the bedchamber from the main hall swayed slightly. He parted the rough fabric and entered. Brenna stood before him. So regal, yet still the girl he grew up with. And the woman he fell in love with.

"Jarl," he greeted her, bowing.

Her laugh was gentle. "You do not need to bow to me, Vali."

"Oh, but I do." He rose and stepped closer to her. "You are the Jarl of Birca. You are... extraordinary."

"I'm still me."

"I am ashamed to admit it, but I didn't really know you until now."

She frowned, remaining silent.

Vali swallowed the lump that had formed in his throat.

"You are stronger and more courageous than anyone I know. You are wise and beautiful. Kind, but determined."

He closed the gap between them, taking her face in his hands. "You were born to rule. The people... they love and respect you as their leader. They know you will protect them and care for them." He smiled. "I was wrong to think you needed anyone's protection. The gods have laid your path with glory and gold."

Her hands came up to cover his, her deep blue eyes shimmered. "But who will care for me?"

"I love you, Brenna. I always have and I always will. And I'll no longer stand in your way."

"You're leaving?"

"Tomorrow." He told her of Frode's intention to marry Nissa.

Her smile was melancholy. "And then you will return to the sea?"

He withdrew his hands from her face, squeezing hers before letting them drop. "Nei. I need to find my purpose."

"Is it not raiding?" Her brow furrowed.

He shook his head. "Not anymore."

"Mayhap, you could stay here... in Birca?"

"And do what?"

A change came over Brenna's face as she stepped back into her role as Jarl.

"I want Birca to become the largest and most important trading post in the region. We sit at the mouth of the Baltic trade route."

She began to pace as she spoke.

"I wish to negotiate new trade agreements with the east but I cannot do that alone."

"You have many merchants and traders familiar with the east here in Birca."

"I do not know these men."

"You are their Jarl, they will work with you."

"I have much to attend too, Vali. I want someone to oversee this work. Someone I know and trust, who knows the Baltic trade region." She stopped her pacing and looked at him. "I need you."

An unfamiliar heat rose on his skin. *She needs me.* He turned the thought over in his mind, unable to process anything else that had been spoken.

"Please," said Brenna. "Will you consider this?"

He nodded, words continuing to elude him.

She moved in and took his hand in hers. "I know you must leave tomorrow." He watched as she wet her lips with her tongue. "But what of tonight?"

She looked up at him with her wide blue eyes. Desire erupted low in his abdomen. He ran his finger down her cheek and under her jaw. Her breathing hitched and her eyes darkened with hunger.

His hands tangled in her hair, pulling her closer, crushing his mouth to hers.

Tomorrow he must leave, and Brenna must step forward and lead her people. But tonight, he was hers and she was his. No matter where his path lay, whether on land or at sea, their fates were entwined. The gods had deemed it so.

The End.

THE VALKYRIE'S RULE

BOOK 2: THE VALKYRIE OF BIRCA SERIES

Prologue

*T*ingvalla - after the death of Sigurd the Black

Audolf Olvirsson spat onto the sand and watched as the royal party made their way down the docks. Sigurd's displaced army followed closely behind like the fools they were. Blonde hair spilled over the black fur that had, until this morning, adorned the shoulders of Sigurd the Black. His shield was strapped to her back; his spear clasped in her hand. None of Sigurd's weapons had been left with his body; ensuring he would receive no passage to Valhalla.

"Níðingr!" He spat on the ground once more, punctuating his hatred of her.

From Audolf's position on the bank of the fjord, he watched them make ready to sail back to Birca. As the woman stepped up onto the side of the waiting drakkar, she turned in his direction.

Even at this distance, Audolf could see the blood of Sigurd painted across her face. Her declaration of her deeds to men and the gods alike. It was a sentiment he did not share.

"Brenna of Birca, another will decide if you are worthy to carry the shield of Sigurd the Black." He spoke into the wind, hoping his words would carry to the drakkar and strike a warning to those abroad.

Audolf had no intention of pledging his fealty to King Aric or the so-called Valkyrie of Birca. Bloodlust fuelled his veins and their talk of peace bored him. Yet he'd stayed to hear what the King intended. It would be useful information when he returned to the only place he thought of as home: Gyldarhagi.

Audolf was one of the few to know the truth of Sigurd the Black's parentage. The man himself had not known who his father was, believing it to be some nameless karl who took his fill of a slave then left. Which was almost true... except it was not a nameless karl who fathered him. It was Gorm, the warmonger and self-proclaimed King of Gyldarhagi.

Sigurd may have been ruthless and bloody-minded, but there was something in him that made him weak. He craved acknowledgement. From a watchful distance, Gorm had recognised it and sent Audolf to keep an eye on his bastard son.

Audolf knew that despite never meeting or acknowledging Sigurd as his own flesh and blood, Gorm would want to know of his demise. He may want to take bloody revenge on the one who'd taken his life, reclaim Tingvalla and mayhap Birca for his own. And that would mean war and bloodshed. Two of Audolf's favourite things.

Grinning, he picked up his axe and shield. It was time to go home.

To be continued in...
Book 2 of the Valkyrie of Birca series:
The Valkyrie's Rule.
Available now on Amazon

Book 3 of the Valkyrie of Birca series:
The Valkyrie Queen
Coming August 2021

Book 4 of the Valkyrie of Birca series:
The Valkyrie Returns
2021/2022

GLOSSARY

*T*he Valkyrie's Viking is set in the country now known as Sweden. Birca and some of the other towns were and are real places. Others are not. Some of the Norse terms used throughout the book will be familiar - some may not be. Many have been the subject of debate in terms of their meaning and application to the Viking age. For the purposes of this work of fiction, the following words and their interpretations are listed here.

ALLFATHER: Odin - The god of wisdom, war, art, culture, and the dead, and the supreme deity and creator of the cosmos and humans

Asgard: The dwelling place of the gods. Asgard has at least 9 realms, including Valhalla.

Berserker: Berserkers were a group of Viking warriors who went into combat without traditional armour. Instead, they wore animal pelts, typically from bears or wolves; or were bare-chested. They were purported to be the most vicious and bloodthirsty warriors.

Bridal-ale: Honey-based mead drunk at the wedding by the bride and groom, and every night for the next month.

Drakkar: A specialised warship, often with a dragon carved into the bow. Could hold over one hundred men.

Dunga: A useless and unhelpful person.

Einherjar: (Pronounced ane-hair-yah) An army of warriors who have died in battle and are brought to Valhalla by Valkyries.

Francia: France

Fru: The title given to the Jarl's wife

Golden Hall: Another name for Valhalla

Gungnir: The spear of Odin

Hel: The underworld where many of the dead dwell, named after the Goddess Hel, who reigns there.

Horn: The horn of a bovid (antelopes, sheep, goats, cattle, buffalo, and bison) used as a drinking vessel.

Huscarl: A member of the bodyguard or household troops of a Norse king or noble.

Jarl: Chieftain. The role of Jarl could be hereditary or bequeathed by the King.

Karl: A member of the middle class. Karls were freemen and land owners. They were the farmers, the smiths, and everyday people.

Karvi: A small longboat, considered to be "general purpose" ships, mainly used for fishing and trade, but occasionally commissioned for military use.

Longboat: A specialised warship

Midgard: The realm where humans live, the Earth.

Ragnarok: The end of the world of gods and men.

Rassragr: Norse curse word meaning unmanly or cowardly.

Rus: Originally Norse people, mainly originating from Sweden, settling and ruling along the river-routes between the Baltic and the Black Seas from around the 8th to 11th centuries AD.

Skal: (Pronounced skol) A toast. A Skål was a bowl that was often filled with beer and shared among friends so the word became a way of saying "Cheers!"

Shieldmaiden: Female warrior

Sordinn: Norse curse word meaning fuck.

Styrimaor: Captain of the ship; leader of the raiding party

Tankard: A drinking vessel consisting of a large, roughly cylindrical, drinking cup with a single handle. Tankards can be made of silver or pewter, wood, ceramic or leather.

Trencher: A small plate of metal or wood, typically circular and completely flat, without the lip or raised edge of a plate

Uppsala: Home of the Temple of Uppsala and the religious epicentre of Viking culture.

Valhalla: The home of Odin and the destination of warriors slain in battle.

Valkyrie: One of Odin's twelve handmaidens who conducted the slain warriors of their choice from the battlefield to Valhalla.Valkyries were also renowned for being selfless, brave, noble, loyal and dedicated to their people.

Viking: Vikings were the seafaring Norse people from southern Scandinavia (present-day Denmark, Norway and Sweden) who from the late 8th to late 11th centuries raided, pirated, traded and settled throughout parts of Europe.

ACKNOWLEDGMENTS

This book began as an exercise in writing about warriors. It kickstarted a deep dive into Viking culture. Amongst the research and reading, I spent many hours engrossed in *Vikings* and *The Last Kingdom* - time incredibly well spent! However fictional those characters and events were, the fierce men and women depicted in these series inspired me to create my own world of Vikings, Shieldmaidens, Kings, Queens and Villains.

As is the case with most projects, this one stalled. Until Aiki Flinthart, finding herself at a loose end after completing her bucket list and finding herself still very much alive, asked if anyone wanted her to look at a fight scene. The creator of *Fight Like a Girl*, author, martial artist, and all round amazing human being was looking for something to do. I jumped on it.

Not only did Aiki critique the first battle scene in this book, she went on to mentor me and the development of this manuscript from an idea to a story, and into a series.

Unfortunately, by the time my first draft was done, Aiki's

time had run out. But she left me with very clear instructions - *stop fucking around and get on with things, but don't forget to live and enjoy life.*

An extended explanation of Aiki's philosophy can be found in her book, *How to Get a Blackbelt in Writing*. I highly recommend you take the time to immerse yourself in it.

There are lots other people I should thank - but as I plan on writing many more books, I'll be selective.

Jacqueline Hayley, Jayne Kingsley, and Kelly Rigby - some of the best friends a girl could have, especially if that girl is a writer.

Jacqui - without a doubt, you and I will take over the world. You inspire me in every way. You were the first reader of this book and the creator of the kick-arse cover. Your own writing blows my mind and your friendship means the world to me.

Jayne - you are in the top five of the nicest people on the planet. A brilliant writer and artist, and so generous with your knowledge and time. There's something to be said about people who place third in *Selling Synopsis!*

Kelly - teacher, mentor, editor, friend. You really are a superhero. We've been through some trials, often at a distance but always there for each other when needed. You are the best editor in the world and one of my all time favourite people.

Special thanks to Janet King for proofreading and always cheering me on.

Lastly, my own little Vikings - Olivia and Chris. I'm so grateful you've figured out how to feed yourselves, so I don't feel so guilty when I spend too long at the laptop. Love you both to the moon and beyond.

Final shout out to the Romance Writers of Australia.

What a gang we are! Life is so much better when surrounded by like-minded creatives who know how to support each other and drink a bar dry. I'm so happy I found this tribe.

ABOUT THE AUTHOR

Tanya Nellestein is an Australian author who writes gut-churning historical Viking romance, bikie thrillers with a romantic angle that always includes good sex and a happily ever after - eventually.

She is also a freelance journalist, specialising in all things romance. Tanya was shortlisted for the Romance in Media Award in 2020.

If you want to make her day, please leave a review on Goodreads, BookBub social media or through the retailer you purchased the book from. Thank you!

To keep up to date with news and latest releases, subscribe to Tanya's newsletter at www.tanyanellestein.com